The Magic of Chemistry Copy

Gigi Hodge

Contents

⁂

Prologue

Twenty years earlier

R ina did not know how long she had been under water. Her cousin Danny had taught her how to take hollow, dead reeds and use them to breathe. She figured that she had waited long enough. Surely Del and Porter had either assumed she had escaped or drowned. She doubted they would go for help if they believed the latter. Slowly surfacing in the densest area of the pond, Rina did a 360 in a slow, methodical turn.

The good news was that Del and Porter had left. No doubt assuming that they could torment her another day. The bad news was that Luke had decided that today was a perfect day to go fishing in the pond. So with her white uniform shirt completely see-through except for the streaks of mud, Rina climbed out of the pond. "Nice day for a swim," Luke deadpanned. Frustrated, embarrassed, and at a loss for words, Rina just made a grunting sound similar to a rhino that hadn't gotten her way, and stormed off to her aunt's house.

"It had to be him," Rina muttered as she slammed into Tante Dianne's house. "Who darling?" called Tante Dianne and then continued when she saw Rina, "Oh dear."

"It is a long story, with a very unappealing ending … you don't want to know," Rina responded.

"As you wish, but you know I could talk to Nonc Julien. Whatever your issue, I'm sure he could straighten it out in no time," Dianne suggested.

Rina shook her head, "At this point, what I have in mind could mean a long prison term for Nonc Jules and I don't need the added burden of guilt hanging over my head."

"Very well, dear, go wash up for dinner," Tante ordered.

"*Oui tante, on mange quoi?*" Rina replied, switching to French to ask what was for dinner.

"*Courtbouillon, dépêche-toi et prends un bain!*" Tante replied, urging her to take a bath. Rina scurried up the stairs, content that at least she would eat well after her nice hot bath.

Luke had caught a couple of bass at the pond. He fileted them and then wrapped them up in a towel. With his fishing pole and his catch in hand, he started the five-mile walk to his house. Sarah was waiting eagerly for him. "Did you catch anything?" she asked.

"Of course, Sunshine. You think I would let my baby sister starve?" Luke replied as he ruffled her hair. He prepared and served the fish with a healthy salad. "It's not as bad as that," Sarah said, rolling her eyes as she finished her meal.

"I know," he replied, but Sarah was looking gaunt and pale. Luke had taken over the care of Sarah after his dad passed and then, three years later, Sarah's mom had taken off. As step-siblings, they had always gotten along, and Sarah had always relied on Luke. He'd been her brother for as long as she could remember.

"School day tomorrow, Sunshine. Hot chocolate, brush your teeth, and then off to bed," Luke said, trying to sound as parent-like as possible, not that he knew what that sounded like. As usual, Sarah promptly complied.

Once she was off to bed, the quiet quickly invaded the room. Luke considered his options. 1) He could go live his own life and Sarah would be put in foster care; 2) He could keep going as they were now and eventually they would run out of money; or 3) He could get another job. He shook his head and smiled. It was not like he had any options. They had to survive, so job three it was.

As he sipped his second cup of hot chocolate, Luke's thoughts went back to the pond and a very disgruntled and disgustingly dirty Rina. He had thought she was just a kid, Rina from the hill. Yet that shirt plastered to her told him that sometime in the last few years, Rina LeBlanc had been growing up.

He paused to wonder what she had been doing in that pond, in the middle of the day in October. "Damn, I bet that water was freezing." He made his mind up to keep an eye on Rina. Something or someone had made her choose to submerge her body in cold water. There's a story there, Luke thought and went to work on the garage account books, thinking that he would eventually find the real story. But in the meantime, he would watch over Rina.

1

Twenty years later

"Rina, you have to come out with us," Danny, her cousin, moaned. "It is going to be the best Halloween drag show ever."

"Much as that tempts me, Danny, I need to finish these lesson plans," Rina responded, smiling at his Superman outfit.

"You always have to work on lesson plans!" Danny whined in a fine imitation of a 10-year-old boy.

"Yes, that's because the little beasties can smell an unprepared teacher a mile away. I don't like seeing them rubbing their hands together in a Renfield imitation when I walk in the room. It particularly does not bode well in a chemistry classroom, since being *canaille* (sneaky and mischievous ... in a good way) in chemistry could entail blowing up the school."

"Fine, but don't complain to me that you never meet anyone."

"Danny, you are going to a gay bar. I'm not gay. The chances of me meeting anyone there are slim to none."

"Fine, fine. Enjoy your lesson planning," Danny caved. "What do you have planned for the beasties?"

"A trek through Poisoner's Corridor. Just the nonradioactive poisons for this week."

"Excellent. Should I drink only bottled water and bring my own lunch?"

"It wouldn't hurt," Rina smiled. "You know they would never poison you, Danny. By the way, can you give me a ride tomorrow?"

"Sure, what's wrong with your car?"

"I'm not sure. It just started making a very scary noise. I left it at Luke's."

"Oh really. Is this the same Luke Hebert you pined after all through high school?"

"Since he is the only Luke I know with a service station, that would be a yes."

"Interesting."

"No, not interesting, but necessary. Sheila sounded very ill."

"I'm sure Luke will take care of her. I've heard he has a way with women." Danny tried to leer, but the effect was overshadowed by his tights and cape. Rina just smiled.

The next morning Rina got dressed for school. She was wearing her uniform of a gray pantsuit and black shirt. She inspected herself in the mirror. Her curly brown hair was a mass of chaos around her plain, round face. Her lips were always annoying because they were too big for her face. Brown eyes that were nearly black. Creole eyes, Tante Dianne always said. She had Creole coloring. Her *arrière, arrière grandpère* was once the governor of Louisiana, so, as Tante Dianne always told her, they were direct descendants of French aristocrats. Not that it gained her any street cred at school, Rina sighed.

She tied her belt above her natural waist, as per her favorite 'What not to Wear' show, pulled on her black boots, and dabbed vanilla on her pulse points. Not bad, she thought, for a thirty-something spinster. Well, that is what pining for a man will get you … a whole lot of nothing. She looked outside at the partially cloudy sky and added her rubber boots and umbrella to her teaching cart, just in case. "Off to the races," she said to no one in particular, and headed out the door.

She stopped when she realized her car was not in the driveway. That's right, the terrible grinding sound and smoke when you turn the key in the ignition. Poor baby, Sheila needed a checkup. Danny will come, she told herself. After about 15 minutes Rina realized that Danny might have forgotten her, and she went to call Sarah to see if she could pick her up. Sarah pulled up about five minutes later in the driveway.

"Good thing you called when you did. I was almost out the door." Sarah was a petite blond with sea-green eyes. Rina always thought she resembled a pixie.

"Morning, Ms. Rina," Bobby said from the back seat, an eight-year-old male version of Sarah.

"Morning Bobby! Sarah, I can't thank you enough. I forgot, until I walked out my door, that your brother is fixing my car today. I asked Danny to pick me up, but unfortunately, I asked him before he went out dancing last night. Should have known better than to think he would remember me after a night out."

"Not a problem, the high school is on the way to the elementary school. So, what is the lesson for today in chemistry?"

"This week we are going down the Poisoner's Corridor, just the nonradioactive poisons and, of course, we will study at bismuth."

"Why is bismuth special?" Bobby asked.

"Oh no," Sarah sighed. Rina rubbed her hands together and gave Sarah a maniacal look. "Well, Bobby, I'm glad you asked. Curiosity is the hallmark of a scientific psyche. You see, bismuth has many qualities and characteristics that the other elements in the Poisoner's Corridor have except for one difference. Bismuth is really more of an antidote. It actually counteracts many poisons. Nature's own Yin and Yang. It's the key ingredient in Pepto Bismol."

"What's Yin and Yang?" Bobby asked.

Rina smiled again at Sarah, who just shook her head and rolled her eyes. "I'm glad you asked that Bobby…" and Rina proceeded to teach Bobby all about Eastern philosophy.

"I think Bobby has learned more in a 15 minute car ride with you than he has in five years of schooling," Sarah said as they pulled into the Meauxville High parking lot.

Rina grinned. "Thanks Sarah! And thanks for the ride. I owe you."

"I will take it out in babysitting. Although now that you have Bobby in your snare, he will probably burn down the house."

"What, me?" Rina tried to look innocent.

"You are the Pied Piper of science, Rina!" Sarah yelled out her window once Rina had gotten out of the car.

Later that day:

Luke wiped the grease off his hands and shook his head. "Some people just should not own a vehicle," he grimaced as the sludge from the oil pan globbed down from the car.

"I know, boss, but she is an amazing teacher," Sam said, defending the guilty party. "My son now knows that cadmium can create a doomsday device, and that it's also known as '*ité*'."

"She's teaching our kids how to blow up the planet … are you sure that is a good thing?"

"Well, she doesn't give them step-by-step directions, but Jr. is renting 'Dr. Strangelove or How I learned to stop worrying and love the bomb' tonight on her recommendation … saying it wasn't appropriate for school, but it was a great movie."

"You know … Rina used to be a good girl. Now she is teaching about doomsday devices and recommending inappropriate movies to our town's young people. Add to that her apparent disregard for her automobile, and I have to say that I don't think

I know that girl at all anymore. What the hell is '*ité ité*'?" Luke brushed his curly dark hair out of his eyes using the back of his hand.

"Rina is a mystery. '*Ité ité* means 'ouch, ouch' in Japanese. My son said there was a cadmium mine in Japan and that according to the 'environmental protocols of the day' — seriously that is what he said, 'environmental protocols of the day' — they took the cadmium sludge after they mined it and dumped it in the river. The farmers started coming down with this disease that they called '*ité ité*' because it made their joints and bones hurt. Anyway, long story short, it was caused by the cadmium, which was being absorbed by the farmers' bodies in lieu of calcium and spread via the river.

Luke looked awestruck at Sam. "What?"

"I just did not know that you were so interested in chemistry," Luke said.

"It's an interesting story, besides I'm not interested, Jr. is. He comes home every day with stories from Ms. Rina. Ms. Rina says this, Ms. Rina says that. A year ago, I couldn't get him to check out a book, and now he is checking out books and reading science magazines in the library for his chemistry project."

"Hope it's not a doomsday device." Luke countered.

"From your mouth to God's ears!"

Luke smiled and continued working on the car. As soon as he fixed one thing, he saw two others that were broken. He worked on Rina's car until the afternoon. Then he stretched his 6'3' frame and went outside for some fresh air. The fresh air was tinged with the smell of rain. Luke closed his eyes and sniffed. Nothing like the smell of rain on a balmy autumn day.

He stayed outside a bit once the rain came down, his favorite rain. The soft cool rain that drops in the sunlight. It looks like little diamonds falling from the sky and feels like a heaven-sent mist to cool your day. After he had cooled off, Luke went back in to finish working on Rina's car.

2

After school was out, Rina stepped out into the sunshiny Louisiana rain with her new red cowboy rain boots and her ladybug umbrella. While she loved her umbrella, she never should have revealed her love of ladybugs to anyone. Her room was now awash with ladybugs. She had every ladybug desk accessory available, and her attic was stuffed with past ladybug gifts. She mused about what would happen if anyone discovered her obsession with Wonder Woman.

Rina plugged in her iPhone and tapped on Pandora to her favorite channel, Dusty Springfield. The Supremes were crooning 'I Hear a Symphony.' She began to sway and sing along as she splashed down the street. Every once in a while, she would do a *pas de Bourré* or sloppy pirouette. She couldn't sing or dance well, but she loved to sing and dance.

That was what Luke saw when he glanced up from the mess of an engine he was working on — Rina splashing, spinning, raising up her arms and singing really, really, really badly. Only the song had changed to the Jackson 5 singing 'I'll Be There'. He tried to stay annoyed. He tried to think of all the damage Rina had done to her car, but he had to fight valiantly to keep the corner of his mouth from quirking up in a lopsided grin.

When she broke out into singing lyrics about always being there, he lost the battle and smiled. Rina's brown curls had turned into a frizz of curls around face and down her back. She was oblivious to the mud covering her slacks and sprinkled on her shirt. Completely content, with a big, goofy grin on her face, she sparkled.

She was in the middle of her rendition of 'What the World Needs Now is Love, Sweet Love,' when she saw Luke. Her smile deepened. She waved and started walking towards him. Luke wiped his hands and went to meet her. "Hey, Luke!" Rina bellowed.

Luke reached over and gently pulled her ear buds out and yelled back. "Hey Rina!"

"Oops, sorry about that. So, how's Sheila?"

"Sheila?"

"Yes, I brought her in this morning for you to cure. She was making a funny noise."

"You name your car and then treat her like that?"

"Hey, I feed her. I exercise her."

"She's a mess … Why am I talking about your car like it is a person? If your car were a person, I would have you arrested for abuse. It's criminal neglect!"

"Okay … sorry … geez. Were you able to cure her?"

"If by cure you mean clean all the fluids out, change all the gunked-up filters, and change all the belts, then yes."

"Ahh … All that sounds expensive. Well, Sheila has been a good car. I'm sure she's worth it."

"I gave you the educator's discount."

"Really, thanks Luke. You always take care of me."

"That will be $500 dollars."

"What?! How much would it be without the discount?"

"$550."

"Gee thanks … I don't suppose you need any tutoring in chemistry or geometry."

"No."

"Hmm … Okay … here is my down payment," Rina said as she counted out $50.

"What am I supposed to do with this?" Luke complained.

"Don't whine. I'll pay you your money. I just can't pay for it all at once. Can I have my keys now?"

"Sure," Luke said as he tucked the money in the front pocket of his jeans, "as soon as I get the remaining $450 dollars." He turned and started working under the hood of another car.

Rina sighed theatrically, "Luke, I need my car to work so I can make money and pay you."

"Not a problem. Sarah can come by and get you on her way to work."

"You can't just volunteer your sister, Luke. What if she has plans?"

Luke rolled his eyes, pulled out his phone, and pushed a button. "Sarah, hey. Would you mind picking Rina up in the mornings and dropping her off at school? Her car is going to be in the shop for a while." Ten weeks more if she keeps paying at this rate, he thought. "No, I can bring her after school. She just needs to get to school."

Rina straightened at that. She did not need Luke to bring her home. She did not want Luke to bring her home.

"Great, thanks Sarah. How's Bobby? Yes, tell him he and Nonc Luke will be hanging out tonight," Luke glanced at his watch and then up at Rina. "Bowling? Yeah, I can make it. I'll ask her. No, I'm not putting her on the phone. Listen Sarah, I have to go. No, she doesn't. I just know that's how. I'm hanging up now ... I'll see you both tonight. Get ready to be shamed by my bowling prowess. You can stop laughing now. Bye."

Rina was grinning like a maniac when he got off the phone. "So how is my old treehouse buddy? Did she have a good day?"

"She is amazingly exactly the same and her day was wonderful, since it started off well." Luke gave her a wink.

"I still remember the first time you brought her over for me to babysit. I told you I didn't know what to do, and you said, 'put her in the tree house and bring her food and dolls'. It was an effective process. It worked for nearly two years until she was tired of dolls and then I switched to Nancy Drew, Hardy Boys, and the Bobbsey Twins. I can remember her sending books down on the pulley system we rigged up. Tante Dianne was so hopeful that I had turned literary. Until she found out the truth."

Luke grinned, knowing the story but asking anyway, "And how did she find out the truth?"

"You know, that's not important. Boring story really."

"Humor me."

"Take $50 off the cost."

"Done!"

"I knew I should have asked for a better story discount. Fine, here is the story. I had just sent up basically the last mystery novels in the house. I think it was a load of Raymond Chandler and Arthur Conan Doyle books. Anyway, I sent them up to Sarah and went to the basement to play with my new bottle of ammonia. I knew I had to keep it away from acids, especially bleach ... however, I did not realize what would happen when it encountered iodine. So, while Tante Dianne thought I was taking books into the tree house to read, I was busy blowing up the basement. There wasn't that much damage. Nothing, a deep cleaning, a coat of paint and a couple days of airing out couldn't fix." She took a deep breath and finished her story.

"Meanwhile, Sarah didn't even know anything had happened. Tante Dianne had gone to the basement, dragged me upstairs, called an ambulance ... which was a bit of an overreaction, I have always thought. Anyway, on her way back from the hospital, she noticed that the light was still on in the tree house. When she went to investigate and there was Sarah, reading all of her books. They have been fast friends ever since."

"And you?"

"Had minor burns and had to figure out a way to rebuild my lab without Tante Dianne knowing. In the end, I took over

Nonc Jules' shed. It worked out perfectly. Tante Dianne, the posh branch of my family tree, found a fellow reader in Sarah and you actually got an adult to watch her. Plus, thanks to Nonc Jule, the sketchy branch of my family, I learned how elemental metals can change chemical reactions when he insisted I learn how to distill whiskey."

"What?!"

"The price for secrecy. I still make him a stash every year."

"Is that next week's lesson in chemistry?"

"God no, next week we are doing what Sam Kean calls 'Fear and Loathing in the Lanthanides'."

"Gonzo Chemistry?"

"You bet. They are the elements that 'lie hidden', so you need to go to extremes to find them. We won't be resorting to illegal substances, though. We don't even get to use real lanthanides," Rina said, trying to sound forlorn.

Luke smiled, not buying it for a minute. "That's too bad."

Rina did the eye slide and mouth twitch that told Luke she was figuring out another tack. "You know, you have some cars here that appear to be just for parts."

"That's right. I sell car parts for money. Parts from cars that are left here or," dramatic pause, "the cars of people who don't pay their bills."

"Don't you dare sell a single fender of my Shelia! I told you I would pay you. I'm on a fixed income."

"Well, of course not Rina. I would never do that to you. Just as I'm sure you would never abuse our friendship by not paying for services rendered in good faith."

"Will you cut that out? Of course I'll pay you. Now, back to the car parts."

"Were we discussing car parts?" Luke asked. "I thought we were discussing chemistry."

"Yes, we were, and you were saying how sometimes you have parts you don't need."

"Was I? You do realize that all the parts that come out of a car must go back in. There aren't any useless parts. What kind of parts would I not need?"

"Oh, say an old catalytic converter."

"Rina, those can sell used for over $300 dollars."

"But who is going to buy them? Wouldn't you rather donate them to science?"

"Will you be using it for a doomsday device?"

"Of course not. I would need cadmium and plutonium for that. There aren't any car parts with those elements, are there?"

"No, and if there were, I would not tell you. Why do you need a catalytic converter? Is it to create an explosion of some sort?"

"No, this is for children, Luke. I try to avoid blowing up other people's children."

"A whiskey still."

"NO!"

"Pity ... you never know when you will need some good whiskey."

"My whiskey wasn't good. It was just really, really, really strong. Besides, I only made that because of extortion. It was the price I paid for Nonc Jules' silence. You know all about extortion."

"Asking someone to pay for something is not extortion, Rina, it's capitalism. The American way."

Luke thought he heard Rina whisper "*les américains,*" but she only smiled at him and said. "Luke, you are missing the point."

"The point being?"

"That you should give me a catalytic converter so my Gonzo chemists-in-training can find what lies beneath the cerium and see the lanthanides."

"I know I'm going to regret asking this but, how are you going to find the lanthanides on the cerium in the catalytic converter?"

"Using our spectroscopes, of course. Then again, lanthanides don't really emit light like other elements. Hmm, perhaps with a chemical reaction."

"My head hurts. How in the hell was Meauxville High able to afford spectroscopes?"

"We made them, silly."

"Okay ... time to go home. My head is going to explode."

Rina examined at Luke quizzically. Then she shrugged her shoulders, threw her bags in the back of his old Ford truck, and went to sit in the seat. Luke got in and turned on the radio.

3

"Can I listen to my Pandora?" Rina asked, pulling out her phone.

"Does it work when you are on the road?"

"Sometimes. Let's try it out. We can do a sing-a-long!"

Luke rolled his eyes. "Oh joy! Which channel?"

"Dusty Springfield, who else? I guess we could listen to Shakira or Lauryn Hill."

"Rap?"

"Hip-hop, Lauryn Hill has a powerful voice. She talks about important social issues facing kids today."

Luke shook his head. "Too deep. Let's stick with escapism."

"Dusty it is." Mary Wells singing 'My Guy' came on and Rina started belting out her off tune version. Followed by Gladys Knight and Pips taking that 'Midnight Train to Georgia'. Rina's voice was even worse in the confines of Luke's pickup. But her enthusiasm was contagious. Pretty soon, Luke found himself humming along and thinking about living in a simpler place and time.

Luke looked over to Rina, her wet curls plastered to her face, and her head back as if she were on that midnight train. He smiled and swayed to the music. Halfway to Rina's, he pulled into the Myran's Maison de Manger (House of Eating) to get some milk shakes. Rina snuck in a "chocolate malt" before she sang "You don't have to say you love me" along with Dusty.

Rina closed her eyes and swayed as she sang in her own little Pandora world.

Luke watched her, smiling as he waited for the shakes. He stayed watching her as she drank her shake, trying not to sing with her mouth full of chocolate malt. They left on the Ronettes singing 'Be My Baby'. And Luke thought, if only, and then he sang with Rina, wanting to give her kisses.

When Luke dropped Rina off at her house, she leaned over to give him a peck on his cheek, and Luke inhaled the scent of sugar cookies. He never could disassociate Rina from sugar cookies. "Thanks, Luke, although I say this is payback for your extortion. Until I get my car back, I will subject you to my Pandora sing-a-longs."

"You have me shaking in my boots, Rina. What channel tomorrow?" Luke grinned, sure of himself.

"Don't look so smug Hebert, tomorrow is Annie, and that means Broadway Musicals."

Luke rolled his eyes. "You're spending too much time with Danny."

"That is a stereotype and I will have you know Danny abhors Broadway musicals. I force him to listen to them for his own good. Like I'll force you to listen tomorrow."

Luke shook his head, smiling, "Nite Rina."

"*Bonne nuit,* Luc," (Good night, Luke) Rina called back as she closed the door.

"Sarah?!" Tante Dianne called down the stairs. "*C'est toi?*" wondering if Sarah had arrived.

"Non, Tante, *c'est juste moi.*" 'Only me', Rina thought and reminded herself to call Sarah to come early tomorrow so she could visit with Tante Dianne.

"You came home with that nice Hebert boy. Send him up to visit with me," Tante Dianne called down. More like to flirt, Rina thought and apologized. "*Désolée* Tante, he already left. He was just dropping me off because he's fixing my car." And extorting money, Rina added to herself. "Sarah will come by tomorrow. You can visit with the better Hebert then. Perhaps she will bring the best Hebert with her when she comes by."

"Oh, *cher tit'* Bobby (darling). You think she will?" Tante Dianne sounded both anxious and exuberant. Rina's lips quirked. Tante Dianne loved, more than anything, spoiling children. She was probably planning the complete takeover of the child's affections as they spoke. Rina knew her approach. Praise, bribes, games, stories, and that's all she wrote. Tante Dianne was always the favorite.

"Why don't I call her up and ask?" Rina asked.

"You do that, dear. Now tell me about your day," she said as she came into the kitchen. And Tante Dianne charmed her all over again. She put out Rina's dinner and told her she had a date at the club. Tante Dianne sashayed out of the house in her party dress and pearls, looking twenty years younger than she should, and Rina just wanted to hug her.

After dinner Rina called Sarah to make sure she hadn't been coerced into picking her up and to secure a visit for Tante Dianne. Sarah answered on the first ring. "Hey Rina, are you coming?"

"Coming where?"

"Bowling with Luke, Bobby and me. Luke said you could come."

"Uh ... I would love to, but like Luke told you today, I don't have my car."

"Not a problem. I'll send Luke over to pick you up."

"Oh ... great ... I think. Sarah, can I ask you a question?"

"Sure, shoot."

"Did Luke railroad you into picking me up in the mornings? I know you have a lot on your plate. I can get a ride from someone else if it is too much trouble."

"Don't be silly. I'd love to come see you and my Tante Dianne."

"Oh yes, Tante D was insisting that you come by soon. Apparently, she wants to start a book club."

"Yes!! She said she might. I have some friends that are dying to meet her. Will she be up when I come by to pick you up in the mornings?"

"That woman wakes up with the roosters. I think she likes to search the house before anyone wakes up."

"Search the house?? Is Tante D still looking for the silver?"

"Why yes, she is Peaches," Rina said in her best southern belle.

Sarah chuckled. "I guess I shouldn't tell her about Bobby's new metal detector."

"God, yes, you must, but make sure I am in the room when you do."

"You crack me up Rina. Listen, I'll be there by 7:45 tomorrow morning. In the meantime, I will send Luke to pick you up, so at least there will be one person I can beat at something."

"I'm happy to be your designated loser. I'll see you and Bobby soon."

4

The knock at the door came as soon as Rina ended the call. "Coming!" she yelled down the stairs. "That was lightning fast!" Rina stated as she opened the door.

A bulky, muscled arm pushed her against the wall as skinny Del sidled past her. "Well, good evening, Rina. What propitious timing we seem to have. Kind of you to have invited us into your abode. Perhaps you could enlighten us as to the whereabouts of your lovely aunt?" But Rina couldn't speak, since Porter's arm was lodged against her windpipe as he held her against the wall. In fact, her vision tunneled due to air loss.

Remembering her 'Miss Congeniality' lesson, she managed to kick Porter in the knee, but she still couldn't dislodge him and reclaim the air flow to her lungs. She began to flail wildly.

"Porter, she needs oxygen to respond to my questions. Kindly remove your arm from her windpipe." Del scolded his partner. Porter let her go, and she dropped to the floor, coughing and rubbing her throat.

She shot Del an aggrieved look and surreptitiously dialed 911 on the phone that she had yet to put away. "Can I help you, Del?" she said snidely.

"Well now, Rina, you just must address an issue that has arisen regarding your mother's estate," Del pontificated. "Del, you are not my lawyer. In fact, you are not a lawyer, so how could you know anything about my mother's estate? I think it would be a good idea if you leave. If you do, I won't press charges against Dumbass over there for attempted murder."

"Pshaw, my dear, he barely touched you. It would at most amount to aggravated assault. As to how I know about your mother's estate, let's just say, I have a plethora of cousins to keep me informed."

"Why, why, why do you always speak to me as if I am an *enfant,* Del? We are the same age. Just speak like a normal person!"

"Normalcy is for the plebeians, Rina. Now, as I was explaining, Porter and I need a modicum of cooperation from you. We need to discuss the terms of your mother's will."

"We don't need to discuss anything, Del, except that you are trespassing on private property and that I am kindly asking you to get your ass off my land."

"Now Rina, you know I detest vulgarity, particularly in a female. Isn't that right, Porter?"

"Sure Del. It t'aint right." Porter agreed.

"Precisely. Now if we could get to the matter at hand."

"Sure, get off my land." Rina announced forcefully.

Porter's hand snaked out and smacked her across the cheek, causing her head to hit the door with a heavy thunk. Rina slid down to the ground in a daze. As her vision tunneled, Rina heard a ruckus at the door and heard what she thought was Luke's voice. And then she saw black.

"Rina ... sweetie, wake up. I'm going to kill them, Bradley. Rina, honey, come on ... get up." Luke lightly slapped her cheeks to get her to wake up.

"Now Luke, I am an officer of the law," Bradley Trahan, the local sheriff, said, "You are not supposed to be telling me things like that. I've already made a call to their probation officers to let them know what happened. As smart as Del thinks he is, I can't believe he didn't notice Rina had called us. We have the entire conversation on tape."

"Hubris." Rina croaked.

"Rina! Are you okay?" Luke shook her shoulders. "It was hubris. That is why Del didn't realize I had called 911. He just assumed he had outsmarted me. Did you catch him?" Rina whispered while rubbing her neck.

"No. What's wrong with your neck?" Luke took her hand away and saw the red marks that Porter's fingers had left around her throat. "Jesus H. Christ, Bradley, they tried to strangle her." Bradley took one look at her neck, called back the probation officer, and then put out an APB on Del and Porter.

Rina tried to stand, but Luke was still holding her. She decided she liked where she was and decided not to fight it. Then she thought how pleased Tante Dianne would be with the situation ... at least as it stood now. Then she bolted up. "Tante Dianne!! Is she alright? She didn't come back while they were here, did she?"

"It's okay Rina. She's fine. She was over at her friend's house playing *Bourré*. We checked on her when we got the call that something was up at the LeBlanc house. Bradley, will you call and let her know Rina is okay?"

"Sure thing." Rina was still dazed, Luke thought, when she started mumbling something about pearls and the country club. Bradley pulled out his phone and then once he said that Rina was alright, he couldn't get a word in edge-wise. "Yes, Mrs. Leblanc. I'll let her know ... I'm sure that is fine. I'll be sure to tell her. Yes. Yes. ok, *bon voyage*."

"*Bon voyage*?" Rina frowned.

Bradley conveyed Tante Dianne's message. "Mrs. Leblanc said she didn't feel safe in the house now that it has been violated and she wants to go down to Florida for a while to visit your

Nonc Jules. She asked me to make sure you did not stay in the house alone. She is worried about you."

Rina pulled away from Luke and sat up gingerly. "Let me get this straight. Tante D is worried about staying at the house, so she is going away?"

"Correct" Bradley said.

"She realizes I can't leave, but she wants someone to come and stay with me to keep me safe?"

"Correct."

"I don't suppose there was someone in particular that she selected. Someone say ... that was male." Rina narrowed her eyes, instantly recognizing Tante D's ploy.

"Well, actually, she asked that Luke stay with you."

"Really, well that is a surprise. If I didn't know better, I would say the entire scene was staged by my aunt, except that she would have never let anyone hurt me. Ow!"

"What's wrong?" Luke asked.

"I think Porter split my lip when he backhanded me," Rina said.

Luke's hands fisted, "He won't hurt you again Rina. I gave Tante D my word."

"No, you didn't. Bradley spoke with her, not you."

"I spoke with her when you were unconscious on the floor from your concussion that you got from the home invasion that happened when you were home alone." Luke's jaw firmed. "So Rina, you have a choice. You can come stay with Sarah, Bobby, and me or I move in here." At that, Bradley looked the other way and pretended to be very busy.

"Excuse me? Did you just give me a teacher's choice of you living with me or me living with you?"

"A teacher's choice?"

"Yes, a teacher's choice is one where the options are limited so that you feel you have a choice, but really you have just been given the option of A) doing what I want you to do or B) doing what I want you to do."

"Well then, yes, you have a teacher's choice—me here or you at my house."

"I choose neither. I will stay here, and you will stay at your house. I'm an adult, Luke. You can't tell me what to do."

"Fine, then I will stay here."

"You can't stay here. This is private property, and I haven't invited you to stay here."

"Watch me." Luke said and pulled out his phone. "*Tante Dianne, C'est Luke. Oui elle va bien (Aunt Diane, It's Luke. She's good)*. Listen, I agree with you, and I don't think that Rina should be here alone. Absolutely, you are right. I think she should stay with me or perhaps I should stay here. I mean, she was strangled and hit. We both agree that she needs some protection. Since Sarah and I were planning to bring her to and from school while she is waiting on her car, I think it would be the easiest way. Yes, ma'am. Absolutely. Thank you for the invitation." He winked at Rina with a look of triumph. "I'm not sure, ma'am, but there is no doubt in my mind they were after something. Something that they did not get yet."

"Something to do with Mama's will," Rina interjected. Luke looked at her for an instant. Bradley noted that tidbit of information in his notepad.

"Rina says it is something to do with your sister's will. Yes, that would be great. In the meantime, you know what those two morons are like. If they hatched a plan, they will see it through. Yes, ma'am, I will do that. No, I will make sure she doesn't leave my sight except to go and teach. You have my word. Yes, here she is." Luke held out the phone to Rina, who glared at him. Luke tried valiantly not to gloat, as Rina swiped the phone away from him.

"*Oui Tante Dianne. Mais j'ai pas ... Mais je veux pas... (Yes Aunt Dianne, I'm not... I don't want to ...).*" However, arguing with your French Creole aunt was fruitless, so she capitulated. "*Oui, oui* okay, c'*est fait. Je t'aime Tante. Tu vas me manquer. Bisous (Fine, it's done. I love you and will miss you)*." Rina kissed into the phone and sent her love to Tante Dianne, but glared at Luke as she pressed end call. "Really, blackmail and intimidation in one day. That's quite a feat, Hebert."

"I do what I can," Luke responded graciously.

Bradley grinned, "Blackmail, intimidation, strangulation, and assault, it has been a banner day for you, Rina. So, do you need me to drive you to Luke's while he goes and gets Sarah and Bobby?"

"Oh crap. I forgot about them. So, what'll it be, Rina? Are you moving into my place, or am I coming over here?"

"I'm not moving anywhere." Rina folded her arms and looked mulish. Luke just smiled.

"Okay ... where do I stay?"

"I don't care if Tante D said you could stay. You can't move in here. Think of my reputation. I'm a teacher, in a small town in the south. I can't be living in sin."

Luc's head perked up. "Will we be sinning? If we will be sinning, I have a few more things to pick up." Bradley laughed as he went out the door.

"Bradley, wait. Bring Sarah and Bobby here, will you?" Rina requested.

"Why?" Luke asked.

"Because we will not be sinning and if they move in, then it won't look as bad."

"Fine." Luke said, not looking nearly as dejected as Rina hoped he would look. Then he gave her that *canaille* look and said, "But I still say that you should give sin a chance."

"Ew, idiot!" Rina tossed a pillow at him and flounced upstairs to prepare guest rooms.

"Hey Bradley." Luke called. Bradley stopped with an aggrieved sigh. "Can you pick up some pizza for us when you go pick up Sarah and Bobby?"

"Sure thing. I'll let Bobby choose the toppings as punishment for your and Rina's abuse of my friendship."

"You're the best." Luke waved to him and went to find Rina.

5

When Bradley went to pick up Sarah from the bowling alley, she was shocked to hear about the events of the evening. Still, he met with some resistance when he suggested he whisk them away to Rina's house. "But we haven't even bowled a game. What about my car? I need it to get to work," Sarah whined.

Bradley was expecting resistance from Bobby, not Sarah. "How about this? I will bowl a round with you while we wait for the pizza. If I win, you let me take you to Rina's house without any whining. If you win, then you can whine the whole time."

"When did you learn to make teacher's choice options?" Sarah asked. "I thought that was a classified teacher's secret."

"Rina was upset tonight and she let it slip. Besides, it was Luke who gave her the teacher's choice options, so it can't be that big of a secret."

"Luke? What were the choices he offered her?"

"I believe they were: You move in with me or I move in with you." Bradley told her.

Sarah smiled. That Mona Lisa, I'm-up-to-something smile that he used to watch her make in high school. The one that boded ill for anyone who was suckered into watching out for her, namely himself. "Don't do that," Bradley said.

"Do what?" Sarah asked as innocently as she could.

"Whatever it is you are planning that makes you smile like that," Bradley said.

"I don't know what you are talking about," Sarah said primly. "I have to make a few phone calls."

"It's nearly your turn, Mr. Bradley," Bobby stated.

"Okay … so tell me, Bobby, is your mom any good at bowling?"

"Not when she doesn't have her favorite ball." Bobby pointed and grinned conspiratorially.

"I see. So if she happened to misplace that ball?"

"Then I would get to order an ice cream sundae with that pizza and you would get to tell my mom what to do."

Bobby's smile, a mirror image of Sarah's, didn't worry Bradley because he knew what it meant. Bradley picked up Sarah's ball and asked, "What would you like on your sundae?"

"Fudge, peanuts, bananas, and caramel," Bobby replied instantly. "You got it, kid. You bowl your set and I will be right back," Bradley said, and he went to hide Sarah's ball and order pizza and ice cream.

"Listen, we need to get a plan," Sarah whispered into her phone. "You know, I have been trying to work this out for years."

"Since about eighth grade," Angelle said. Her eye roll was apparent in her voice. "Sarah, I really think you should just let nature take its course. What happens will happen … yadda yadda yadda and throw in some more platitudes."

"No, you've got to help me out, Gelli. You know all about this stuff," Sarah said.

"Well, you must know something about this stuff. You do have a child," Angelle retorted. The silence stretched out and

Sarah swallowed and then forced herself to ask. "Are you going to help me or not?"

"Of course I will help you. Am I not your bestest friend?"

"Yes, yes, you are," Sarah said, relief in her voice. "So the question is, how do we keep them together for the maximum amount of time? I could stay with you," Sarah volunteered.

"Ah no."

"Why not? Bobby and I are very good housemates."

"Yes, but Luke will wonder why you don't just go home."

"Good point."

"Plus, if you leave, then they might not stay together."

"I have a feeling you were asked to stay over there to keep tongues from wagging. If Rina is worried about her reputation, then she won't do anything reckless, and we need some reckless behavior from her to get us to our ultimate goal."

"Exactly. So, I stick it out over there, but make myself as scarce as possible."

"Well, you and Bobby have a busy week planned."

Sarah's smile returned. "We do, indeed." She said as she walked back to the bowling lane.

6

R ina was upstairs putting clean linens on all the guest beds when Luke caught up with her. "You feeling alright?" he asked.

"Fine, fine, I just have to get all the rooms ready for you." Rina brusquely started putting the sheets on the bed and Luke stepped to the other end of the bed to help her.

"You know, it is not like we are guests. You can simply throw the sheets on the bed and we can take care of it."

Rina's look told him what she thought of that remark. She nearly snapped a pillow through the pillowcase. "It is not that," she stated. "I just don't like being railroaded into having you here. You always seem to be the one to get me out of binds. It is like my entire childhood. I could never get away with anything because you were always there to make sure that trouble never even came near me."

"It was the pond diving." Luke stated.

"Excuse me? Pond diving? What are you talking about?" Rina asked.

"When you were 15 or 16, I was out fishing at a pond. It was a chilly day in October or November. Suddenly, you rose up from out of the pond with your school uniform covered in mud and your hair covered in flotsam and jetsam. You said something pithy and went home and I just couldn't figure out what would make an intelligent girl go diving into cold pond water in the middle of fall. I had to figure it out. It did not take me long to figure out that Del and Porter had targeted you with their stupidity."

"Was that why they suddenly stopped picking on me? And here I thought it was because they were afraid they killed me in that pond. Well, it seems they are no longer scared off by the 'Invincible Hebert'," Rina smiled when he winced.

"God, do NOT call me that. I swear I almost wanted to throw an interception just to lose the moniker."

"Poor baby." Rina intoned. "It's tough dealing with all that adoration. Although, how you played sports with all those side jobs, I will never understand."

"I'm a multitasker. Besides, I think being a football star gave me many perks professionally."

"Yes, I can see how it would be beneficial at the Dairy Queen, or with your tutored students."

"I always was allowed very flexible hours."

"Yes, but you were still limited to the requisite 24. That must have been difficult."

"Nah, you took care of the hard part."

"Me? I never helped you with any jobs."

"You made sure Sarah was safe and happy."

"She was just a few years younger than me. I really just considered her like the younger sister I never had. Plus, after the basement explosion, it was really Tante Dianne who took care of Sarah."

"Right." Luke said and went to place the sheets on another bed. "That was why she always came home with stories of 'Rina this and Rina that'. I swear she was going to perm her hair and dye it black." Rina chuckled. "I kid you not. She tucked in boxes of both brown hair dye and perms whenever we went grocery store shopping." Rina tried holding back her laugh, tears coming to her eyes. "What's so funny? I had to check the cart every time she came shopping with me. It got to be such a habit I still check my cart for hair dye and perms."

This time Rina could not hold it in. She fell back on the bed and exploded into tears and chuckles. "I'm sorry," she said between laughs. "I'm just trying to picture fine, blond and straight-haired Sarah with a dark brown perm. Add to that the image of your digging through your grocery cart for contraband each time you shop. You have to admit, it's funny," she chuckled.

"Marginally," he said and smiled. God, she loved that smile. Rina quickly looked away, rolled off the bed, and tried to focus on the task at hand. "I need to get to work on dinner and then my lesson plans," Rina said, trying to uncharge the atmosphere.

Luke, to diffuse the sudden tension, changed the subject. "Bradley is bringing pizza when he brings Sarah and Bobby. So, you can go and work on lesson plans. I'll call Sarah and let her know what I need to spend the night."

Rina escaped to her room to work on her lessons. Once she left the room, Luke exhaled. Being in a room with Rina on the bed and laughing while she grinned up at him was disconcerting. It took all his self-control to keep from jumping on the bed and joining her. Good God, how was he going to survive this? Luke lay down on the made bed and tried to think about something else ... anything else. Well, at least his sister would be here soon.

"You cheated!" Sarah fumed, as she climbed into Bradley's patrol car.

"I don't know what you are talking about and frankly, I'm insulted that you would even think that I cheated. I beat you fair and square lady. Just ask your son."

"The son who is gorging on a chocolate sundae as we speak? I don't think so. And if you are so upstanding, then what happened to my lucky bowling ball?"

"Sarah, I'm shocked that you would distrust us."

"Don't even try. I know the schemes Bobby pulls to get his hands or rather tongue on some sugar."

"Well, if you hadn't read 'Sugar Blues'..." Bradley said.

"I hate that book," Bobby chimed in, as he did each time anyone mentioned the title.

"If you hadn't read 'Sugar Blues', maybe Bobby would not be so easy to influence."

"Let's agree to disagree, shall we?" Then Sarah turned to Bobby. "You will need clothes for at least a week, Bobby. Bring your baseball gear as well. Nonc Luke can work with you while I return to my tree house."

"Your tree house?" Bobby asked, avid curiosity in his voice.

"Yes, when I was growing up, Ms. Rina always let me play in the tree house. She hid me there for the first few months that she watched me and used to sneak me food and books."

"Fun!"

"I know, right? It was even more fun once she blew up the basement, because then Tante Dianne found me, and I got even more books!!"

"Ms. Rina blew up her basement!" Bobby sounded impressed.

"And her bedroom and the chemistry lab at the high school, both as a student and once as a student teacher." Bradley added.

"Wow," Bobby was in awe. "How did she do that?"

"With what she calls the 'Magic of Chemistry'," Sarah said with a flourish, just like Rina always did. She grinned, remembering the first time she had heard 13-year-old Rina discuss the 'Magic of Chemistry'.

"Do you think she'll teach me?!" Bobby asked.

"Unfortunately, I'm sure she will happily teach you. That is what she does. She is the Pied Piper of chemistry."

"Huh?" Bobby was confused.

"Don't they teach you anything in school? Haven't you read fairy tales?"

"No, but we did a test prep once on fairy tales, and I was able to create a constructed response without knowing one thing about them. Mrs. Lewis was very impressed."

"I'd be even more impressed if she actually taught you something."

"You work at the school mom, why don't you teach?"

"Because Mommy did not have the foresight to stay in college, sweetie. Learn from my mistake, Bobby. Stay in school."

"You should go back to school," Bradley interjected.

Sarah stiffened. "Oh yeah, and how could I do that? I have responsibilities. I have to work, you know, and then my nights are kind of busy."

"I could watch Bobby some nights, so you could take a class. We could work on his homework and his 'Call of Duty' skills."

"Really! Oh, Mom, you should go back to school. It would be an excellent example for me."

"Go back to school so that you can play an M-rated video games? Don't think I don't know about video game ratings, Bradley. I don't think so."

"Fine ... so we will play a different game. A teen-rated game and homework ... Come on, Sarah. You would be a great teacher."

"You think?"

"Absolutely, I don't know anyone who lectures as well as you do," Bradley said with a smile.

"Thank you ... I think. Was that a compliment?"

"Just think of all the things you can change. Instead of test prep, you could teach something frivolous, like math." Bradley winked at her and pulled into her drive. "Here we are. Do y'all need help packing your gear?"

"No." Sarah said, "We can do it," but she was thinking about her dream and wondering.

7

R ina worked in her room. She had gotten the students' attention with the Poisoner's Corridor and the lanthanides. Now she wanted to keep it. "And now for something a little bit different," she said as she sketched circles, trees, and other items on black construction paper and attached them with a tab on the floor. She worked on getting the large flashlight to have them cast shadows on some butcher paper she had affixed to the wall. She was adjusting the light when she heard from behind her.

"I hesitate to ask this, because I know I will regret it, but what do circles, trees, and birds' shadows have to do with chemistry?"

"The noble gasses."

"Seriously, that is your answer. You are saying it as if it makes perfect sense."

"Plato described this allegory of the cave, in which he says that everything that we know is nothing more than a reflection of a perfect ideal. The birds we see are not perfect birds, but a reflection of birdness. He believed that all creation is working towards that perfection. He also says that we are incomplete entities, always searching for that missing part of us. This is true of atoms also, nearly all atoms are missing some electrons and searching for something to make them whole. Except for the noble gasses, they are their 'idealness'. They have that perfect octet in their outer electron ring and thus they need no one to make them perfect. They are ideal or noble."

"So everything in creation is looking for missing parts of themselves?"

"According to Plato. We are all just out there trying to pull away electrons missing from our makeup. That is why I always smile at the English term 'pulling' when they talk about looking for an evening companion. It seems so apt."

"I don't know Rina, you seem to embody the perfect Rina-ness." Rina blushed and smiled. Then she thought of that missing piece and wanted to escape. She heard a thump from below. "I think that was the front door."

"Saved by the bell, are you?" Luke smirked.

"Yes, indeed. I'll race you to the door." Rina darted out of the room and Luke ambled after her, wondering about Rina's missing electrons.

Sarah, Bobby, and Bradley arrived at the door with suitcases and pizza. Sarah and Rina went to set the pizza on the kitchen counter, and Luke, Bobby, and Bradley carried suitcases up to the rooms.

"Take any available room you want," Rina called up to them. After she set down the pizza, she went to her room to finish lesson planning while her guests settled in.

"I want one that looks out on the tree house!" Bobby exclaimed.

"That would be Rina's old room, before she blew it up," Luke replied.

"Cool ... is it still blown up?"

Bradley smiled. "I doubt it Bobby. Tante D was hardly one to allow a room to remain in anything other than impeccable condition. So … Luke … how did you know which room used to be Rina's?"

"I used to come here to pick up Sarah after work. Tante D couldn't be bothered to keep track of the 'ruffians', as she termed Sarah and Rina, so I would just search the house and the tree house for them when I came by," Luke smiled. "I can't tell you how many experiments I blundered into. Rina must have gone through a 100 chemistry sets."

"Can I have a chemistry set, Nonc Luke?" Bobby asked, hope in his voice.

"For all the gray hairs Sarah has caused me, you can have two."

"Woo-hoo! Wait til I tell Mom."

"Let's surprise her, shall we? Ms. Rina and I will go out and find an appropriate chemistry set for you later this week. Then Ms. Rina can teach about the periodic table of elements and where on the table you can find 'Poisoner's Corridor'."

"Cool!! She talked about that in the car earlier. Pepto Bismo is what she calls an antidope. It stops poisons, but it is still in the Poisoner's Corridor because of some Japanese ping-pong."

Luke shook his head and tried to decipher what Bobby had said. "Do you mean yin and yang?"

"That's what I said," Bobby explained. "It is all about balance. She said there is always balance in the world."

"Yes, there is. Now go out and play in the tree house like your mom. You want a book?" Luke asked.

"A book?"

"Yeah, a book filled with pages and those funny characters that have meaning. Your mom always had a book when she went to the tree house."

Bobby went to the bookshelf in his temporary room and scanned the shelves. "This one looks interesting," he said.

Luke looked over his shoulder and read aloud, "'The Alchemist's Handbook: Manual for Practical Laboratory

Alchemy', by Frater Albertus. Sarah will appreciate that one. However, that might be a bit over your head. Try this book." Luke reached over for a bright red book with the word 'Alchemy' on it. "I think that was one of Ms. Rina's favorite books growing up. It is a wonder she did not blow up the entire house. Okay, you have your book. Now, off to your mom's tree house."

"I thought it was Ms. Rina's tree house."

"Nah, once Sarah started coming over, she turned it over to her. She said that it was better to have stone and concrete around her. Apparently, as she stated, 'the elements in stone are not as variable or mutable as the elements in wood.' Secretly, I think she enjoyed knowing that Sarah had a space. She considered your mom her adopted baby sister."

"Does that mean I can call her Tante Rina?"

"That's between you two. Now off you go. We'll call you for dinner."

"Thanks, Nonc Luke."

"You're welcome."

Bobby scurried down the stairs, slammed the door, and Luke saw him run to the tree house. Luke grimaced a little when the ladder rope swayed, but relaxed once Bobby got inside and slammed the door.

"Sarah needs to work on that door slamming," Luke said, partly to himself.

Bradley put his hands in his pocket and wandered around the room. "So, how does it feel to be back?"

"Bradley, I've lived in this town all my life. If you haven't gone anywhere, you can't really come back. Can we please talk about something else? You've been a pain in the ass since you got your minor in psychology."

"Double major Criminal Justice and Psychology. I aspired to be an FBI profiler."

"How did you end up in Meauxville?"

"Like you, I never left, except for college. I have a deputy who will make it, though. Deputy Landry did a profile on Del for me."

"So what does his profile on Del say? Should we be worried?"

"Yes, but I need to speak a bit more with Rina. You sort of whisked her away before we could talk."

"I know she said that Del said something about her mom's will."

"I'll see if Mrs. Sally can email me a copy." Bradley said, as he pulled out his phone.

"Mrs. Sally is still at work?"

"No, but she can hack into the system from her house."

"Sweet dear Mrs. Sally is a hacker?"

"Best hacker in Saint Marc Parish. She could legally access the information from the office, but Mrs. Sally enjoys working from home and I think she likes that it is *verboten*."

R ina lay on her bed with her chemistry and lesson books spread around her. Luke peeked in and asked, "You hungry?"

"Starving ... is everyone eating already?" Rina asked as she yawned and stretched. Luke tried not to notice that she was stretching on her bed. That her breasts looked round and soft and that it did not look like she wore a bra when she was in her PJs.

"Ah ... no, just gathering everyone to eat now. I still have to get Bobby in from the tree house."

"Yay! The tree house is back in business." Rina jumped off the bed and threw Luke a big smile. "Did he get a book?"

"'Alchemy' by E.J. Holmyard."

Rina rubbed her hands together and gave the maniacal look Luke was familiar with. "Excellent, another convert to the 'Magic of Chemistry'."

Luke ruffled her curls and smiled. "The 'Magic of Chemistry', I remember when you tried to convert me. You should have shown me the moonshine whiskey recipe."

"I only use my knowledge for good." Rina tried to look virtuous.

"You know, maniacal seems like a much more natural look for you. You don't do virtuous very well."

"I beg your pardon?" Rina affected an affronted look.

"If chemistry doesn't pan out for you, don't waste your time on theater. You will never make it big."

"Oh, really?" Rina raised her eyebrows and then slowly sashayed over to him. "You think I don't have it in me?" She whispered in his ear, her soft lips brushing against his cool ear shell. Rina pulled back to look at him. Their eyes locked and Luke's burned into hers. For a moment, there was only heat. Then Rina giggled, pushed him onto the bed, and then slammed the door as she ran from the room.

Luke took a few minutes to cool off on Rina's bed. Not that being on Rina's bed was helping him to cool off. Counting to 20, he straightened the papers on Rina's bed and headed downstairs to eat, or at least pretend like he was eating. Pizza would not assuage his hunger.

He called Bobby's name out the window and saw Bobby try to climb down the tree house ladder while reading his alchemist's handbook. Sarah is going to kill me, he thought ... or she'll kill Rina. That second thought perked him right up.

8

Rina made an executive decision to eat the pizza at the kitchen island rather than the formal dining room. She pulled up one of the five stools and sat on it.

"Change of plans?" Luke asked as he grabbed the stool next to hers.

"The dining room was too stuffy. I didn't want Bobby worried he would damage the 100-year-old table cover. Plus, I feel taller when I have a stool."

"Yet, you still seem tiny to me, Squirt," Luke said.

"Stop it, you know I hate that nickname." Rina argued.

"Ah ... just like old times," Sarah said as she came into the kitchen, interrupting their argument. "You are too short," she said to Rina.

"And you are too tall," she said to Luke.

"And you, my sweet, are just right," Bradley told Sarah, giving her a big, loud kiss.

"Ewww gross!" Bobby scrunched up his face. "We are going to be eating. Stop doing that stuff."

"Sorry kid," Bradley said, slipping him a Hershey's kiss.

"You can't keep bribing him with sweets. He is not supposed to have sweets," Sarah said.

"Sorry, it is just that he gives me that pathetic, 'I never get to eat chocolate' look and I feel for him. Bobby, show her the look." Bobby channeled abandoned puppies and gave Bradley the most pathetic, downtrodden look he could muster.

"Wow," Luke said, "I want to give him a Snickers bar. I almost feel compelled to do it."

"You missed your calling, kid. You oughta be in show business." Rina said.

"Turn it off, Bobby." Sarah told him. "Here, have some pizza, fat and simple carbs, your favorite." Bobby smiled at his mom, and she smiled back and ruffled his hair. "Eat," she said. Sarah looked at Rina. "I had forgotten the size of this kitchen," Sarah said. "I remember when Miz Comeaux used to fix us snacks after school and we would come in here and tell her about our day."

"Is that Tante Dianne's maiden name?" Bobby asked. "No, we told Tante D about our day after we were fed, and had washed our hands and faces and combed our hair. Mrs. Comeaux was Tante D's housekeeper. We got to talk to her with filthy hands and faces and hair, although she made us wash our hands before we ate."

"I remember her chicken and sausage gumbo on the first cold day of fall," Luke said. "I would come to pick Sarah up after work and Mrs. Comeaux would fix me a bowl, along with some potato salad and garlic bread. Suddenly, this pizza doesn't taste as good."

"I want some gumbo," Bobby agreed.

"It is not cold yet," Rina told him. "You have to wait for the first cold day of autumn before you can have some gumbo. So, for now there is pizza and a tree house. When it gets cold, it will be gumbo and the playroom."

"You have a playroom?" Bobby asked, interested once more.

"With pool, ping-pong, and an old PS3 Move, so Ms. Rina can get her exercise or murder Mr. Danny in 'Call of Duty Black Ops'."

"Cool!" Bobby said and threw a surreptitious glance at Bradley.

"Don't even think about it," Sarah warned. "No 'M-rated' games."

"You certainly have a lot of rules, Sarah," Bradley said, "but you know what they say about rules."

"You lot are impossible. I'm going to take a bath and you do what you want, but you," she pointed at Bobby, "better be in bed when I get out of my bath." As soon as she left, everyone abandoned their chairs and scurried to the game room.

"How much time do we have?" Bradley asked as he popped in the 'Call of Duty: Black Ops' CD.

"At least an hour," Luke said. "I just picked up her latest historical romance. She usually reads the entire thing in a single bath."

"God, I love a book in the bathtub. Only problem with all those electronic books. They aren't waterproof," Rina said. "What is she reading?"

"Laurens somebody." Luke said, "I play Bobby first."

"Stephanie Laurens, regency, nice choice," Rina said.

"I know nothing. I just pick up the books when they come out." Luke said.

"Less chatter and more play," Bradley said. "I wanna play the kid before it is his bedtime."

After dinner and game time, Rina cleaned off her bed and laid back down on it. Exhausted from the day's events, she instantaneously fell asleep. Luke went through the house saying, "goodnight" and turning off lights when he noticed Rina's lights were still on. He knocked, but there was no answer. "Rina, you okay?" he whispered through the door. Still no response. Luke eased the door open and found Rina fully dressed and lying on top of the covers.

Luke grinned down at her until he saw the handprint bruises on her throat. Then he just fumed. Unwilling to undress Rina, he knew his self-control would not hold. Luke pulled off Rina's shoes and tucked her under the covers. Rina smiled in sleep and cuddled into her pillow. Luke kissed her on her temple and Rina's lips drifted up. Brushing her hair off her face, Luke moved away from the bed, turned off the lights, and closed the door.

"Any news from Mrs. Sally?" Luke said, sitting down at the kitchen table with an evening cup of coffee.

Bradley sipped from his cup and slid some papers over to Luke. "It is right here, but I don't see anything that could cause Del to want to hurt or intimidate Rina."

Luke's fists closed tightly, thinking about Rina's bruised neck. "Can you get your dad to have a look at it? We need to figure out what Del discovered, if he discovered something."

"Sure." Bradley responded. "Dad loves Rina. I think she has been making whiskey for him. He'll figure out what Del found. And he definitely found something. Del is an idiot, but he is not stupid."

"So you're heading out?" Luke asked.

"No, I think I'll just stay here. If Del or Porter come back, I don't want Sarah or Bobby in harm's way."

"Yeah, I didn't want them here either, but Rina would not come to us, and Sarah practically leaped at the chance to stay over here. I guess she missed this place more than I thought. She practically grew up here." Luke took his and Bradley's coffee cups to the sink to rinse them out.

"Yeah ... I'm sure that was it," Bradley rolled his eyes and then went to lie down on the couch in the family room across from the kitchen.

_9_

Bradley was just getting comfortable on the couch when Sarah walked into the kitchen in her fluffy robe and slippers. He watched as she got out the milk and the chocolate syrup and two mugs. "I want some too." He said from the couch, making Sarah jump in surprise.

"*Fils d'putain* (son of a bitch). You scared me! What are you doing lurking about?" Sarah looked disgruntled.

"Language, language. You don't want to teach Bobby just the bad words, even if they are the only words that you know."

"*Piqué toi (FU),* Bradley!" Sarah retorted. Bradley lifted his brows in surprise.

"Wow, I taught you well!"

At that Sarah grinned, "You did, didn't you? Too bad 'bad French' is the only French I know. You want some hot chocolate?"

"Yes, please, with whipped cream if you have it." Sarah pulled the can of whipped cream out of the fridge and smiled at Bradley. The image short-circuited his brain for a moment, but he recovered quickly. Sarah began to test the whipped cream by foaming some on to her fingers.

"On one condition." Sarah stated as she licked the whipped cream off her fingers.

"Name it." Bradley said, thinking, 'anything you want'.

"You tell me why you are sleeping on Rina's couch."

"Well, I thought that if I were sleeping in your bed, others might object, saying that I was a bad influence on Bobby."

"Ha ha, I would object." 'Not,' she thought. "I'm still waiting on the actual explanation," Sarah continued, while putting the milk in a saucepan and pouring in the chocolate sauce.

"Well, the thing is that Luke is here to make sure that Rina is alright."

"I know. Did you see those bruises? She will have to wear a turtleneck to school tomorrow."

"While Luke is here to make sure that Rina is alright," Bradley continued a bit louder, "I am making sure that you and Bobby have someone watching over you."

"That is so sweet. You are such a good friend, Bradley," Sarah exclaimed as she stirred the hot chocolate.

'Oh yeah! Friendsville', Bradley thought to himself. Exactly where I don't want to be. Bradley got up to sit once again at the kitchen table.

"So, do you think Rina still likes him?" Sarah asked.

"Who?" asked Bradley.

"Luke of course."

"Yes." Bradley said.

"And?" Sarah prodded, pouring the hot chocolate into the mugs.

"And what? Sarah, you do know I'm a guy, right? You're aware of that?" Bradley sounded perturbed.

"Of course I know. I just wanted to discuss Luke and Rina with someone. It's not like I could talk to Bobby." She slid the hot chocolate in front of him.

"Because Bobby is a boy and boys don't like talking about relationships. Neither do men, by the way. We dislike talking about relationships unless there is a guarantee of sex." Bradley took a sip of the hot cocoa, "Are you giving me that guarantee, because if so we can discuss all the minute signs that point to Luke and Rina's possible attraction to each other. I like the girl on top, by the way. If you are debating the sex guarantee ... just a little incentive. Cuz I know you're a take-charge kinda girl."

"You are a dog!" Sarah said as he foamed whipped cream onto his hot chocolate.

"What?! Why? I'm just trying to hold a conversation here," Bradley smiled, took his hot chocolate, and went back to the family room couch. He purred, "Well, you know where to find me if you want to 'talk'." He made a quotation marks sign with his hands, leaned back on the coach, and took a sip with his eyes closed. Sarah made a strangled sound, grabbed up the two remaining cups of hot chocolate and went up the stairs to deliver the hot chocolate to Bobby and chat with him.

"**S**o Sweetie, how was school?"

"We already talked about school, Mom, remember at the bowling alley? I told you everything I know."

Good grief, Sarah thought, it's a testosterone thing. "I know, but we were interrupted by news of the attack on Rina."

"Did you see her cool bruises? You can see the fingerprints on her neck."

"Since those fingerprints were caused by someone trying to hurt and possibly kill her, I would not mention the 'coolness' factor to her."

"You're probably right."

'You think?!' Sarah thought silently.

"You should see this awesome book I got from the library, Mom. Nonc Luke said I could take it up and read it in your tree house."

"Be still my heart. My son is reading and in my tree house. It's a miracle. So, show me the book." Bobby took the book out from under his pillow and presented it to his mom with a flourish.

"It is the coolest book. You should see all the illustrations. It even talks about alchemists from all over the world."

"Sooo, 'The Secret Garden' didn't appeal to you?"

"What are you talking about? Why would I want to read about a garden? Look! Islamic alchemists and here, Chinese alchemists ... this is a seriously cool book."

"No 'Bridge to Terabithia'?"

"Mom, I don't want to read that stuff. It is boring."

"Fine. Tante Rina for the win. Now, finish your hot chocolate, turn off the light, and go to bed." Sarah kissed Bobby's temple and turned off the overhead light.

"K, night mom." Bobby took his last sip, turned off the bedside lamp and laid back in his bed.

"Oh, and don't forget to brush your teeth!" Sarah called back as she walked down the hall.

"Aww." Bobby got up and went to do his mother's bidding.

Meanwhile, Sarah started to turn to her room. Then she thought of Bradley lying on the couch to make sure she and Bobby were safe. She also thought about the whipped cream and how hot his eyes got when she was testing the whipped cream. Sarah quietly snuck into the kitchen, grabbed the can of whipped cream and then leaned over Bradley on the couch.

Bradley opened his eyes. "You wanna talk?" he asked. "No," Sarah said and tossed him the can. "I wanna 'talk'" she made the quotation mark gesture with her hands, planted a big wet kiss on his lips and ran out of the room. Bradley smiled and thought, 'screw Friendsville', and followed Sarah out of the room.

Rina thrashed around, trying to escape her nightmare. She struggled against the pressure at her throat. She cried out and arched off her bed. The scream woke up the entire house. Luke flew into Rina's room to find her fighting her nightmare.

"Oh Darlin'," Luke grabbed her and held her from behind. Rina fought, thrashing and whipping her head around until Luke started kissing her temple and stroking her shoulders. Rina just started sobbing then, still caught in the nightmare. After she had cried herself out, she simply slumped against Luke and fell back asleep.

Luke hadn't noticed that Sarah and Bradley had run into the room after him. Once Rina went back to sleep, he looked up and saw Sarah. "Do you need anything?" she whispered. "No, I'll just stay here. In case she had another nightmare." He whispered back. He settled Rina into the bed under the covers and slid in next to her over the covers, pulling her into his arms.

Rina snuggled and squirmed for a few minutes and then fell back to sleep. Luke sighed. I'm going to go to straight heaven for this good deed alone, he thought. Rina was soft and warm in his arms. Her curls were soft and smelled like cookies. Her breathing was soft and rhythmic, and Luke eventually fell asleep curled around her.

10

"Well, that was an inauspicious start to this venture," Del sighed. Porter just watched him and pretended to understand.

"Luke is always around. Remember when we were little, and you always had us picking on Rina? Luke seemed to always show up then, too," Porter interjected.

"He is a noxious rodent interfering in my plans, and he will be crushed." Del hit his fist into his other hand as he said it.

"Del, aren't rodents usually small? Luke is big — he is almost bigger than me," Porter interjected again.

"He will be crushed, nevertheless. You will take care of that," Del responded.

"I will? How?" Porter turned his head to the side and looked exactly like a confused puppy, a very large, confused puppy.

"You will simply corner him and beat him to a pulp. You know the routine. It is your *modus operandi* and your *raison d'être*." Del ground out from between his clenched teeth.

"My what? You know I never took any of them foreign languages, Del."

"Just beat the shit out of him, Porter. That's what you do," Del said, exasperated.

"Oh ... well, why didn't you just say that?" Porter questioned.

Del started pacing, then stopped to examine the will again. He knew he wasn't wrong. The money was his only if he could get his hands on Rina. Plus, there were the items in the will that specifically went to Rina. He knew that the lost silver had to be in those items, which meant he just needed to get his hands on them.

"So we just go in the house and take them, right Del?" Porter asked. He was chaffing to get out of their cheap motel room and do something.

"*Imbecile. T'es bête!*" Del muttered in French.

"Now, Del, you know I don't speak that French. Speak in English!"

"Imbecile, you are an idiot. Is that better?" Dell asked.

"It is true what they say. Things always do sound better in French," Porter mumbled. Del grinned. Porter was amusing, if nothing else.

"So, back to the plan. I have this list of five items from Rina's house. My hypothesis is that these items will give us clues as to where all that silver is stashed." He did not mention the rest of the plan to Porter. He did not need to know about that.

"How much money Del?" Porter inquired.

"Pots and pots." Del responded.

11

Rina woke up and felt warm and snug. Rina also felt a warm breeze through her hair. It was very relaxing, and she did not want to get up, but she knew that her natural tendency to lie around in bed was why she would never see size six again. Oh well, double digits were more interesting, and she could always pretend that her size was a base five number, which meant in base five she was a size seven.

Smiling at her new sizing strategy, Rina went to grab her shoes for her morning walk and realized that she was being held in place. She looked down to see a large hand on her stomach and a muscled arm wrapped around her waist. Feeling a bit disoriented, she turned around to see Luke cuddled around her and breathing through her hair. Rina quickly thought back. She remembered lying on the bed exhausted, but not much after that.

She nudged Luke awake. "Luke," she stage whispered, "Luke, get up." Luke slowly lifted his lids, lowered them, and pulled her closer to him. Rina lingered there for a little while, just taking in the feel and scent of him. "Luke," she whispered again, "I need to get up." Luke started to move his hands from her waist down her hips and then started moving them up her body. "Luke!" she whispered loudly.

"Can't blame a guy for trying." Luke said with a grin.

"You are a moron," Rina said and tried to get up off the bed. Luke was still holding on to her. "Let me up!"

"Alright, alright, just give me a second to wake up. Where are you going anyway at this god-awful hour? There is no way you have to get up at 5 a.m., just to go to school at 8." Luke rubbed his hands over his face and stretched. Rina tried to ignore him but ended up just staring at him. "Well," Luke said.

"Huh, what?"

Luke smiled. "Why are you getting up now?"

"Oh ... I have to walk Sherman." Rina got up and dug around in her bureau for some sweats. She pulled out the ugliest pair of sweats Luke had ever seen. Luke was grateful that she was trying to change into some ugly clothes, because he was having a hard time forgetting how Rina felt in his arms last night.

"Who is Sherman?"

"He is just a dog that started showing up every morning when I went for my walk. He looked hungry, so I started feeding him." Rina looked around for a place to change. She slipped inside the closet and put her sweats on.

"Bad idea. If you feed them, they keep you." Luke said, rubbing his hands over his face. He was swinging his legs off the side of the bed and getting up when Rina re-emerged from the closet.

"I don't want him to go away. I love Sherman."

"Nonc Luke, what are you doing in Tante Rina's room?" Bobby walked in with his Alchemy book and a quizzical look on his face.

"Ahh," was all Luke could muster.

"Umm Nonc Luke just came in to speak to me Bobby," Rina ad-libbed.

"Why was he laying on your bed?" Bobby asked.

"Ahh ... because he was trying to mess up the covers after I just made the bed," Rina improvised.

"Very nice." Luke whispered, tucking his hands behind his head, enjoying Rina's discomfort.

"My friends do that when they sleep over," Bobby empathized. "You know what the best thing to do when someone does that is?" Rina caught the twinkle in Bobby's eyes.

"No." she smiled, "What is one to do when a ne'er-do-well keeps messing up one's neat, well-made bed?" Rina saw the slight weight shift, read the writing on the wall, and smiled at Bobby as they both projected themselves onto the bed in tandem. The "oof!" was loud and rewarding. As Rina and Bobby sat up in a fit of giggles, Sarah knocked on the door frame.

"Bobby, quit tormenting Nonc Luke."

"*Merde*," Bobby muttered under his breath.

"Bobby!!!" Sarah exclaimed, shocked, while Luke and Rina erupted into a gale of laughter.

"I told you he would learn the curse words," Bradley said from somewhere in the hallway.

Sarah turned in mock fury, "You!! You taught him that word. I can't believe."

"Not me," Bradley responded, his hands up in the international gesture of "It wasn't me." Sarah turned and looked at Luke who was laughing underneath a smirking Rina, who was trying desperately not to laugh.

"Rina, you keep tormenting Luke. We are going down to discuss our LANGUAGE." And with that, Sarah stalked downstairs. Bobby followed, but first he turned and winked at Rina and said,

"Sometimes you have to pay the consequences, but it really is the only way to retaliate." Rina had to laugh then. Tears streamed down her face and her jaw ached.

Luke's amusement, however, had faded when Rina, who had been sitting on top of him, started to wriggle with laughter. He eventually had to pick her up and set her beside him. He struggled to remember that they were not dating and that his sister, nephew, and best friend were downstairs. As Rina recovered from her fit of giggles, Luke eased off the bed and ruffled her hair (which shut her up immediately) and went downstairs to join his family.

Rina's body, warm and tingling from the laughter and proximity to Luke, now thrummed with unquenched need. Story of my life, she thought. She went to walk Sherman and then got ready for school. Picking up her lesson plans, she headed down to get some coffee and something to eat.

"Tante Rina," Bobby exclaimed after she sat down at the table and filled her plate with pancakes. "What's on the agenda for today?"

"Bobby, you do know that Rina is not officially related to you," Sarah whispered to him.

"I know, but she will be," Bobby whispered back with surety. Sarah smiled, and Luke cleared his throat. Ignoring the byplay, Rina explained that everyday she walked Sherman and then taught her chemistry classes. "What about alchemy? Will you be teaching about alchemy?" Bobby asked.

"No, about the..."

"Magic of Chemistry!" Rina, Sarah, Luke, and Bradley exclaimed together.

Bobby giggled. "No really, what are you studying today?"

"Don't get her started," Luke said. "It will make your head hurt."

Rina elbowed him as she slipped on her light sweater for her walk. "Besides Plato, which might be over your head, we are studying the healing properties of sulfur. Well, actually, we are studying how sulfur acts like birth control to bacteria."

Bobby snorted. Sarah was not amused. "Rina, that is hardly appropriate for an 8-year-old."

"All I'm saying is that sulfa drugs don't kill bacteria, they just keep it from reproducing," Rina responded.

"Well, why didn't you say that?" Sarah asked.

"Because I teach psychosexual teens, and one of the sure ways to get their attention and get them to remember things is to bring up the topic of s … er… reproduction."

"Lord, is this what Bobby has to look forward to in his education?"

"Yes," Rina said. "You know, if you don't like the state of education, there is one thing you could do."

"What?" Sarah asked.

"Teach!!" Bradly, Luke, Bobby, and Rina said together.

"I have explained, I can't. I work all day and at night."

"At night we can all take care of Bobby." Luke said, "We would love to hang out with him."

"He could read in your tree house." Rina added.

"We could go bowling and I could teach him French curse words," Bradley added. Sarah glared at him. "I mean, I could teach him how to gossip in French," Bradley corrected. "Hey, I can only teach him what I know."

"Please mom!! Please!!" Bobby begged.

"Fine y'all win! I'll call Louisiana University, State Tech, and McNair U today."

"Yeah!" Bobby cheered. "Well, I need to go meet Sherman." With that, he went outside.

"Well, I better go with him since he doesn't know which dog is Sherman and he might start petting the wrong dog." Rina escaped out the door.

Luke just smiled at Sarah. "What?" Sarah asked.

"Nothing," Luke grinned. "If I had known it would just take Bobby hanging in your treehouse to get you back to school, I'd have asked Rina to babysit a long time ago." With that, Luke walked out the door.

Sarah poured herself another cup of coffee and then went to open her laptop.

"So, which school are you going to choose?" asked Bradley

"I don't know. I nearly have enough credits for a bachelor's, but if I go back for education, we are looking at three years of school. I don't know if I can work and go to school for that long."

"Luke wouldn't mind. He would love to take care of you some more while you finish your degrees."

"I would mind. Luke already worked since he was in high school, numerous jobs so that I could stay with him and so I could go to school and then I blew it."

"You didn't blow it. You got side-tracked."

"Yeah, by stupidity."

Bradley's voice hardened. "Having Bobby was not stupid."

"No!! I didn't mean that. I meant what led up to having Bobby. My ... partying."

"Sarah, waking up pregnant after a college party and not remembering what happened is not partying sweetheart, it is rape."

"Bobby is NOT born out of rape! We've had this argument before. It wasn't like that."

Bradley clenched his fists, but relented. "I know Sarah, I'm sorry."

"Don't ever say that! Bobby is the best thing that ever happened to me."

"Yes, and now you can show him what his mom is made of by going back and doing what you always wanted to do."

Sarah smiled, "I can, can't I?"

Bradley returned her smile. "That's what I've been telling you."

"I know, but it is different here. This is the house that made my dreams come true the first time. When I was young, I wanted a mother and a sister. Then I came here and *Chêne Vert* gifted me Tante Dianne and Rina." Sarah's eyes welled up, "And now it is working again, I love this house."

Bradley tried to smile and not envy an inanimate house. 'Change the subject,' he thought, 'that's the ticket.' "Well, I need to get to work. I have dastardly criminals to ferret out."

"If you find Del and Porter, shoot them!" Sarah commanded.

Bradley smiled, "It doesn't quite work like that, sweetie."

"But it can," Sarah called back to him as she took her coffee and went to her room to change.

Bradley called after her, "Do I need to keep you under surveillance?"

"You do anyway," Sarah called down the stairs. 'This is true', Bradley thought, 'this is true', and he finished his coffee and headed to work.

12

Del woke up Porter. "We need Rina to sign the papers, now. We need to figure out a way to get to her."

"Why don't we just go back to her house and ask her?"

"Gee Porter, perhaps because she called the cops and they now know that we are targeting Rina. Plus, she apparently has several house guests now, one of which is our friendly sheriff."

"You think Bradley is friendly? He always seemed mean to me." Del did not feel like explaining the concept of sarcasm to Porter, so he just ignored him and tried to think, only to be interrupted by Porter again.

"We could get her at school. She's a teacher, you know."

Del shook his head and tried to remember why Porter was an asset. "There are too many witnesses at school. No, we need someplace where she won't have anyone around."

"Rina is always around people," Porter exclaimed. "She has lots of friends. She was even nice to me, remember? Even after we chased her into that pond."

"Can we please focus here?" Del retorted. "So we can't get her at home and we can't get her at school. What else does she do?"

"I think we should watch her," Porter said, "Then we could tell when she is alone." Del stopped his cogitation and stared at Porter.

"What?" Porter asked.

"Nothing, it's just that you're right, and I'm trying to adjust to the novelty of that experience."

"Oh," Porter said and smiled, not knowing what else Del had said but hearing the "you're right." And being happy to contribute to his friend. They spent the rest of the day monitoring Rina to see if she ever went anywhere alone.

Rina got home that evening and saw Bradley laying on her couch. She sat down next to him and asked, "Bradley, do you ever get the feeling that you are being watched?"

Bradley froze. "What do you mean?"

"I know it sounds crazy, but I have just had this feeling, all day long, that I've been in someone's sights. I just can't seem to shake it. It went away for a bit when I was in my class, but as soon as I left school and walked to Luke's, it was there again. In fact, and this will sound absurd, as soon as I started walking to Luke's, I felt like that 'looker' was gaining on me. I practically ran to Luke's this afternoon. It's crazy, I know."

"Not crazy. You walk to Luke's by yourself?" Bradley inquired.

"Yeah, he has taken my car hostage, so Sarah drops me off and then I walk to Luke's so he can drive me back."

"Why has Luke taken your car hostage?"

"Well, he wants me to pay him for work that he did to make it run again. Plus, he wants to flagellate me for taking such awful care of the car, which I admit is true. I always think that since I barely drive it, I don't really need to take care of it."

"How much do you owe? I could loan you the money."

"No, I need to pay for it myself. If I don't suffer the consequences, how will I learn from my mistakes?"

Bradley grinned, "Spoken like a true teacher."

"I'm going to have a glass of wine, to get rid of that creepy, I-know-what-you-did-last-summer feeling. Do you want something?"

"Another beer?"

"You got it. Is Sarah around?"

"Upstairs looking at universities."

"I'm SOOO excited about that! I can't wait. I still have all my textbooks and notes."

"Of course you do." Bradley smiled.

"What? She might need them. Plus, if she goes elementary, she will need me for her science methods course."

"I don't think you can talk to 8-year-olds about how Sulfur keeps bacteria from reproducing."

"See ... you remembered!"

Bradley smiled and conceded defeat. "That is true. I can't seem to get the image of sulfur condoms from my brain."

"Visual learner," Rina intoned, and then went up to see how Sarah was getting along in her university search.

Sarah was not just searching on the computer, she was surrounded by printed programs and, in true Sarah fashion, had begun a list of pros and cons for each program.

"So, what have you researched thus far?" Rina asked. Sarah looked up, relieved to see someone who would understand her dilemma.

"I need to work Rina. I know that Luke said he will take care of us, and you said that we could live here indefinitely."

"It really is as much your home as it is mine. I promise, Sarah, Tante Dianne always wanted you here. It is even in her will."

Sarah stopped at that. "What?"

"Tante Dianne always felt that you truly understood the property and that you truly appreciated the house."

"I love this house. I always feel like I'm home when I'm here."

"Exactly, that is why Tante D wants you to be part owner once she can no longer able to care for the property."

"But it's your house. Tante D is your aunt."

"Yes, but she was more like your mother, and I think that she also left you half of it to make sure that I wouldn't blow up the place. Before she left for Florida, she said, 'Well, at least Sarah will be there to watch over *Chêne Vert'*."

Sarah's eyes welled. "I will, you know. Take care of it, that is. I'm so glad Bobby is getting to stay here, too."

"I think he likes it as well. However, I will warn you that now that he has come over to the dark side, you might have to work to keep both of us from blowing up the house."

"I know, of all the books in your library, he chose the 'Alchemy' book. What are the chances?"

"Actually," Rina quipped, "He chose the 'Alchemist's Handbook', but Luke thought it would be too difficult for him to read. If he'd read that one, he would have probably been overwhelmed. Lucky for you, Luke was there to point him in the right direction." Rina rubbed her hands together and did her best mad scientist, maniacal laugh.

"Thank you, Nonc Luke," Sarah said snidely and continued with, "I'm gonna kill him. Well, he will be buying the chemistry sets. I can tell you that."

"Oh, I have extra chemistry sets." Rina smiled as she walked out, "Well, off to grade my videos."

"Don't you mean papers?" Sarah asked.

"Oh no. I send home experiments that students can do with everyday household products and cheap video cameras, if they don't have smartphones. The kids have to show me each step of the experiment. They need an introduction where they describe the purpose and methods they are using, the actual running of the experiment, and then a final discussion of what they learned. Wanna watch?"

"Yes, how is it you still have a job? You would think some parent would get upset with you blowing up their houses."

"Oh, I don't send scary experiments home, just simple ones. The worst that could happen is turning the kids blue."

Sarah laughed, thinking Rina was kidding, but when she turned, Rina wasn't laughing. "That was a joke, right?"

"Being blue doesn't hurt them." Rina defended.

"You do have liability insurance, right?" Sarah asked.

"Of course. Tante Dianne has it come right out of the trust. She's afraid I'll forget to pay the bill."

"Tante D was always very wise." Sarah shook her head and chuckled and then sat back to look at the chemistry videos.

13

B radley scanned the alley between Meauxville High and Luke's garage. There were countless hiding spots and numerous places to stash a getaway car. He did not like it one bit. Add to that the fact that he had watched Rina dancing from the high school to Luke's, completely happy and completely oblivious to anything around her. It was a recipe for disaster.

He had watched Rina all day, and he had only found two times when she was not around people: 1) when she walked that atrociously ugly but somewhat intimidating dog and 2) when she bebopped her way to Luke's to get a ride home. Since the dog would probably savage anyone who tried to hurt Rina, Bradley had to figure that Del and Porter were going to try to get their hands on Rina during her dancing trot to the garage.

"Listen Luke, I think you should give Rina her car back. I think she would be safer if she could go directly home from work."

"That would be true, Bradley. If you were naïve enough to believe that once she got her car back, she would indeed go straight home," Luke retorted. "I know for a fact that she would hie off to God knows where and do God knows what, completely oblivious to any danger lurking about her."

"Point taken, but we have a problem," Bradley warned him.

"What problem? Sarah takes her to school, and I take her home. We always know where she is. My plan is foolproof."

"Except that Rina walks here from school, with her iPhone blasting in her ears, dancing like a lunatic."

"It's adorable. Have you watched her sing to the Supremes? It is the worst caterwauling you will ever hear, but cute, cute."

"No doubt, but while she is injuring your eardrums, she is also oblivious to the world around her and could easily be taken by surprise by nefarious ne'er-do-wells."

"You realize that as you profile Del, you are starting to sound just like him."

"I'm just saying that we need to figure out a way to keep Rina safe, as she is doing the electric slide over here."

"I'll talk to Sarah," Luke agreed.

"I didn't mean that Sarah should be her shield," Bradley countered, annoyed.

"Never Gonna Happen. Rina would step in front of a bus to keep Sarah safe. As far as she is concerned, that is her baby sister. What I meant is we need to convince Rina; Sarah is the one who can do that."

Rina plugged in her earbuds, slipped on her galoshes and raincoat and started off to Luke's garage. She was listening to the Annie Broadway musical channel on Pandora and singing "It's a hard knock life."

She was just belting out a complaint about getting kicks and not kisses when an arm snaked around her and pulled her backwards. Drawing on instinct and what she learned from her many viewings of Sandra Bullock in 'Miss Congeniality'. Rina stomped on her assailant's instep, kicked her foot up and back to his groin, and then elbowed her assailant in the solar plexus.

The arm was just loosening when Rina whipped her head back to crack her skull into her attacker's nose. The arm released her, and Rina just ran. She couldn't tell if they were following, or if there were footsteps behind her. She might not be lithe, but she knew how to run, and she was fast. Fear added another surge of adrenaline, and she streaked out of the alley.

Del cursed when Porter made it back to him. He inferred that the surprise attack on Rina had not worked based on the fact that Porter did not have her, was limping, and his face was covered in blood.

"Porter, the woman is pudgy, short, and in her mid-thirties. What possible reason could you have for coming back empty-handed? Must I remind you again that I am the brains, and you are the brawn? If you can't live up to your responsibilities, what is your 'raison d'être'?"

"My favorite raisins are the Craisins."

Del took an exaggerated deep breath. "First, let me say. You are an idiot. 'Raison d'être' means your reason for being. Second, and I don't know why I'm telling you this, but, Craisons are not really raisins. Raisins are dried grapes and Craisins are dried cranberries."

"Oh," was all Porter said and then, "well, I like them, anyway."

"Fabulous. Any chance you could spare some of your intellectual energy to figure out what we are going to do now?" Del snarked.

"I don't have to have a plan. I'm the brawn. If I'm the thinker, then you won't get any raisins."

Del did not bother trying to understand; frustration made his head throb even harder.

14

Moments later, Rina came running into the garage; the fear evident in her eyes. Luke tried to wipe off his hands before Rina leaped into his arms. She buried her head in his shoulder and Luke hugged her and then ran his finger through her hair. His hand came back bloodied. Rina just sobbed. He tried to calm her down, but she would not let go and could not stop crying to talk to him.

He mouthed, "Call Bradley" to Sam. As Rina calmed down, hiccupping and snorting against Luke's shirt, Luke couldn't help but smile. Whatever it was, he would take care of it. The important thing was that when Rina was in a jam, she came to him.

He was sitting down now. He had maneuvered her to the chair and sat down with her in her arms. His arms curved around her waist.

"I'm sorry Luke, it's just … it's just it was so awful." She started sobbing again as Bradley flew through the door.

"What happened?"

"Rina's upset about something," Luke informed him.

"Yes, I can see that. What is she upset about?"

"In the alley," Rina choked out. Bradley called into his shoulder radio for his partner to scope out the alley.

"What was in the alley, baby?" Luke asked. "I was dancing and then …" Hiccups and sobs started all over again. Luke tried to guide her through the story. "You got off of school and I assume you put on your earbuds to listen to music?"

"Annie, 'It's a hard knock life'."

"It is indeed. So, you were listening and dancing to Annie and walking to the garage."

"Uhmhumm," Rina mumbled, her face tucked into Luke's chest.

"And then something bad happened?"

"He grabbed me around the throat. Why does he always go for my throat?"

"Who?" Luke asked, his fists bunching and flexing.

"I think it was Porter again. It felt like Porter and smelled like Porter. He always smells like a hamburger dive."

"So Porter grabbed you around the throat, but you did not see him?" Bradley asked, trying to make sense of the entire scene.

"His arm came from behind and wrapped around my throat. I couldn't breathe ... again. This is getting annoying." Rina griped while wriggling free and looking perturbed.

"Crap, he must have a hundred pounds on her. Rina, sweetie, how did you get away?" Luke asked, troubled.

At that Rina grinned, "SING," she said, "solar plexus, instep, nose, and groin. Although, I went with the instep, groin, solar plexus, and then the nose. Although the head butt to the nose hurt like the dickens. I think I hit his mouth."

"There's blood," Luke mouthed to Bradley.

"You know, I can see you in the mirror. If there is blood, I don't think it is mine. I hit him VERY hard," Rina said, sounding proud of herself.

"Well, let's take you to the doctor, just in case, to get you checked out," Bradley said.

"I'll drive her," Luke stated. "Sam, take over here, will you?" Sam, who was looking troubled at the door, just nodded.

"Crap," Sam said, "I don't know what Jr. would do if something happened to Ms. Rina."

"Nothing is going to happen to Rina," Luke snapped. "Not while I'm around."

Rina was fine. Slight concussion to match the one she had gotten earlier when Porter first attacked her. The blood was not hers, so Bradley took a sample for evidence.

The doctor sent her home with some Zoloft to keep her calm and said to call if anything happens. Luke tucked her into the car and brought her home. When he got there, Bradley had already filled Sarah and Bobby in on the story. He let them know in no uncertain terms that they were never to be alone again doing anything ever ... ever!

Luke had Rina by the hand when he strode inside *Chêne Vert*. He sat her down at the table. His set jaw and firm gaze warning Sarah and Bobby that there would be not be a question/answer session. Rina, however, needed to talk.

"Do you think he'll come back again?" She asked. "If so, maybe Sarah and Bobby should go somewhere else. Hell, maybe I should go somewhere else." Rina lowered her head to the table. "My head hurts again, my throat hurts again, too. I hope I broke his nose."

Somehow, Luke could smile through his rage. "I'm pretty sure you did."

Bobby was nearly jumping out of his seat. "Oh boy, wait till I tell the boys at school that you beat up Porter Douguet."

Rina lifted her head and smiled, "I did beat him up, didn't I? Well, at least there's that."

"Beat him up, girl, you clobbered him," Sarah said, then walked to stand in front of Bradley, elbowing him in the solar plexus. "See, SING always works." Rina giggled, but then held her throat in pain.

Luke's rage grew, but he stamped it down. "We should probably get you into bed." Rina, who had once again laid her head on the table, muffled out a, "Not tired."

Bobby whispered to her, "It doesn't work when you say that with your head down and your eyes closed."

Rina turned her head and smiled at him and said sleepily, "You are so wise. Who are your favorite alchemists?"

"I'll tell you in the morning, Tante Rina. I need to get to bed and so do you." Bobby leaned down and kissed her on the cheek.

"So wise for one so young," Rina snuffled as she laid her face on the cool table top and fell asleep.

"I got her." Luke swooped her into his arms and carried her to her room.

Rina tossed and turned and moaned throughout the night. Luke could not stand it anymore. He grabbed his robe, strode to Rina's door and lay down next to her ... above the covers. As soon as he got in the bed, Rina took a deep breath and sank into a calm sleep.

Later that day, at his new hideout, in an abandoned sugar mill, Del slapped Porter upside his already bruised head. "Are you stupid or something?" Del continued to rant at Porter while he slumped his shoulders with an ice pack on his face. "How could you let an out-of-shape lady barely over five feet trounce you again? Need I remind you," he pointed to himself, "brains," and then he pointed to Porter, "brawn. Why am I bothering with you?"

"I dunno, Del. You already told me this."

"It bears repeating. I'm not even going to bother to explain what a rhetorical question is."

Del paced the bare apartment living room. Then he looked out the cracked window through the filth. "Perhaps we are going about this the wrong way. Perhaps we don't need to bring Rina to us, we just need to go to Rina."

"But Del, Luke, and the sheriff are staying at her place."

"I know that, but they can't watch her all the time. Although, it will be harder to arrive at that moment since your latest screw up. They'll be watching her like a hawk."

"Well, we will watch her some more and see when she is on her own." And that is what they did for the next two weeks. They observed her walking the dog, going to school, being driven home by Luke. They watched her go to the library every weekend and the gym once a week.

"Gonna take more than that to banish those love handles," Del whispered as she walked into the gym.

"I think she is cute. She is all round," Porter defended her.

"Never mind. It has to be with the dog. The only time she is alone is when she is with the mutt."

"That's not true, Del. Sometimes Bobby goes and walks with them."

"I know that Rina defeated you, Porter, but are you really worried about an eight-year-old child?"

"I'm not worried. It's just that he would be a witness, and I'm not roughing up some eight-year-old kid!"

"Porter, sometimes your moral code astounds me. You don't scoff at brutalizing men or women, but you go out of your way to keep kids and pets safe. You are starting to lose your value in this operation."

"I don't care. I ain't touching Bobby or the dog."

"Fine, have it your way," Del said as he crushed the back of Porter's skull with the butt of his gun. "I've never liked to share, anyway."

⚜

15

"**I** think I've figured out why Del and Porter are after Rina. Can you two come by the office?" Mr. Trahan asked. Luke looked across the table to Rina, who was fixing hot chocolate for everyone.

"Who was that?" she asked as she handed him a mug of hot chocolate with whipped cream, sprinkles, and caramel syrup on top.

Momentarily stunned by what he knew would be a heady sugar rush, Luke hesitated. "Bradley's dad. He thinks he knows what the issue is. It is not your mom's will, it is your grandpa's. Wanna head over there?"

Rina grinned over her mug. "As soon as we finish the hot chocolate. It is a work of art, as you know."

"Tell me about it. God, I feel like I'm sinning each time I take a sip."

"You know what I always say, 'if you're gonna sin; sin big'," and with that, she took a huge swig of her hot chocolate, which left a mustache of whipped cream on her lip. Luke took just as hefty a swig, hoping the sugar rush would douse his lust. Then he and Rina headed to Mr. Trahan's law office.

A bell rang as they came through the door. A stylish older woman was at the desk and smiled as they came over to her. "Luke, Rina, he's expecting you. Go on in."

They stepped through the door to find an older version of Bradley, except in Armani, and groomed within inches of his life. "Please sit down. I think I've found the problem and the solution," Hercule Trahan said, gesturing to the comfortable leather chairs.

Twenty minutes later, Rina was up in arms. "So what you're telling me is that Pawpaw hid, what, a dowry in his will? And … and … and," rage made Rina stutter, "and that if I marry someone in a direct line from the original founding families of Meauxville, my husband will get that money. You must be kidding me. What are we in the 18th century?! Women don't come with dowries anymore and blue blood is the color of everyone's blood before it comes in contact with oxygen!"

Luke just sat back and tried not to grin. Rina on a rant had always been a thing of beauty. He remembered bringing up politics at the dining table when they would eat at Tante D's. He forgot how much he loved to see her venting her spleen, as Tante D used to call it. While Luke mused, Rina continued her rant, "So … so …so…"

Besides the cute enraged stutter, when Rina was furious, her face turned red—deep red. Luke grinned, but he averted his face to keep from having to deal with the full force of Rina's rage.

"So," Rina took a deep breath, trying to get her emotions under control. "What you are saying is that Del is trying to marry me."

"He is a descendant, one of the few, of the founding families, both on his mother's and his father's side," Mr. Trahan stated. "But he would need my permission, my acceptance, to get married."

"Rina, there are disreputable people around. He could just kidnap you and then marry you against your will."

"But surely, everyone would know."

"The account is a Swiss account that only requires a legal marriage license to transfer the account."

"So the only way to get him off my back is to get married?"

"Not just get married. You need to marry a descendant from the founding families. Simultaneously, you would need to have a will in place to ensure that if anything happens to you or your spouse or, that money goes elsewhere."

Rina stared, dumbfounded. "You're kidding me. I have to marry some stranger to get Del off my back? Couldn't we just catch him and arrest him?"

"The problem, my dear," said Mr. Trahan, "is that Del has several dumber cousins that are just as mean, but not as bright as him. Word has gotten out that Del is after you and it has something to do with the will. You can expect them to start to either court you or try drag you to the altar."

"Creepy," Rina shivered. "So, what do you think I should do?"

"You need to marry a descendent."

"So, marry and then immediately divorce them?"

"Not exactly. There is a stipulation that you remain married for at least a year, and there is a bonus if you have kids—$500,000 for a boy and $250,000 for a girl."

"I'm going to dance on Pawpaw's grave. I'm going to stomp around and pull out all the flowers and kick over his gravestone!!!!" Rina's face was a deep shade of beet red now.

Luke stepped over to her and put his arm around her. "Relax Rina, let's just hear Mr. Trahan out."

"Fine, fine ... finish it ... please." This was not Mr. Trahan's fault, she reminded herself.

"Well, now, I was thinking," Mr. Trahan drawled, "that you could marry another eligible person. You can then agree to share the money with that person and agree to divorce in a year's time. If that is what you want, I have the papers right here. I am a judge. We could do this now."

"But who?" understanding dawned. "You want me to marry Luke!!!" Rina looked horrified.

"Okay now, I'm trying not to feel insulted. I'm actually considered a good catch."

"No, no, I didn't mean it that way. I'd love to marry you, Luke. I mean, I would have no problems marrying you. I just think that marriage should have other motivations."

"Yes, well, getting Del and his inbred cousins off your back seems like a great reason to marry. Besides, it will keep us from living in sin."

At that, Mr. Trahan's eyes opened wide, and Rina's face flushed bright red. "We are not living in sin. You have a room to yourself!"

"But I slept in your bed last night," Luke added.

"Young Lady! You will be getting married immediately. Your aunt would be horrified if she knew you took up with young Luke here as soon as she left on vacation."

"First, nothing bad happened. We just slept together," commented Rina.

"Yes, no one would describe what happened as bad. Except for the most prudish of people," replied Luke.

Mr. Trahan's face was turning red. He was frantically pulling out the required paperwork.

"Sign here, Luke."

Luke smiled and signed with a flourish.

"Wait, you don't understand. He is just moving in to take care of me."

"The day Dianne's niece becomes a kept woman..." Mr. Trahan held the pen out to Rina and indicated where she needed to sign.

Rina picked up the pen and tried to explain while Mr. Trahan forced her pen to the paper. "I am not a kept woman. I can take care of myself and choose who and when I want to be with a man," she said, enraged, as she signed the paper.

"Not anymore," Mr. Trahan stated, "because by the power vested in me by the State of Louisiana, I now pronounce you husband and wife. Luke, you can kiss your bride."

"What!!! Wait!!! I wasn't thinking. I was just agreeing to a contract, like on the Internet. You know how no one reads those contracts and just agrees. How Bill Gates is now the happy owner of everyone's first child?"

"I'll let your aunt know that you finally tied the knot. About time too. She was starting to worry that you were going to end up a spinster."

"Can we please ixnay on the 18th century speak of dowries and spinsters? Speaking of dowries, Luke is a rich man now, right?"

"I didn't marry you for your money, Rina."

"Oh, for Pete's sake. I wasn't saying that. I just wanted to make sure that when we tell Sarah that you are paying for her schooling, I can let her know that it is okay because, thanks to us tying the knot, you are loaded."

'Of course she would think of Sarah', Luke thought. "You're right. No way out of it for her now."

"Damn straight. If I'm stuck, then she is stuck. So, Mr. Trahan, you cut the dowry in half, right?"

"Absolutely."

"So what am I now worth? I have a spectroscope that is calling my name and we need new lab equipment and chemicals."

"Think four million each will cover it?"

The silence was complete. "I'm sorry, could you repeat that?" Rina asked.

"Four million each. That is what Del was after, the eight million dollars. I also included in the papers new wills for you both. The funds will go to your nearest relatives, Tante Dianne, and your cousin Danny for you, Rina, and Sarah and Bobby for Luke. So now we have taken the wind out of Del's sail. Do you need me to set up a trip for your honeymoon?"

Luke laughed as Rina started and exclaimed, "Not gonna to happen."

'We'll see,' Luke thought as he escorted her out of the office. As they exited, the sleek and stylish assistant flung rose petals at them and wished them well, much to Rina's chagrin.

$$16$$

Luke called Sarah to tell her the good news. Somehow, in the 20 minutes it took them to drive home, Sarah had organized a wedding reception complete with a bride's and a groom's cake, a karaoke machine, and a disco light ball.

Rina was both aghast and impressed. It all seemed a blur as Rina cut the cake, danced with Luke and her friends, and sat down for a toast and an impromptu potluck dinner.

Bradley stood and clinked on his glass. "To Rina and Luke for putting Meauxville out of its misery and tying that knot." Everyone laughed and clinked their glasses together.

"What did he mean by that?" Rina sounded disgruntled. "What misery?" Luke just smiled like a cat who had figured out how to work the cream dispenser. Hours later, after the festivities had wound down, Rina waved goodnight to the last guest and collapsed on the couch. "Well, time for bed," she stated.

"Good idea. I would love to be a fly on the wall when Del gets the news that we spiked his guns," Luke said as he climbed the stairs in tandem with Rina. They both turned down the hall and Rina said one last goodnight as she turned into her room. Luke slipped in behind her as she allowed the door to close and said goodnight as well.

Not expecting him to be so close behind her, Rina whipped around. "What are you doing here?" she asked

"We're married. This is my room now, too." And he edged in closer to her.

"I don't think so." Rina backed away, her eyes flew to the door, judging the distance and trying to formulate an escape plan.

"Uh uh … no escape. If nothing else, we need to sit down and discuss our future."

"We have no future. We will stay married for 365 days and suck it up to the tune of over $10,000 per day and then you will move out, but Sarah and Bobby will stay."

"10,000 per day! Holy shit. Wait a sec. How come I have to leave, but Sarah and Bobby get to stay?"

"Tante D wants them to stay. She said that when I told her you were all coming over here."

Luke looked at her skeptically. "And Tante D didn't want me to stay? Even though I have always lived with Sarah and Bobby their whole lives?"

"Alright, alright, the invitation was for the whole family. You can stay indefinitely. You know you always were welcome here."

"Thanks!" Luke said and jumped backwards onto the bed.

"Welcome in our home, not in my bedroom! Get out!"

"I hate to break it to you, Curves, but I've actually been coming in here every night since Porter tried to nab you in that alley."

"What are you talking about?"

"I'm talking about nightmares, Curves. The ones that kept waking you up in the night with them and you seemed to sleep better in my arms. You do, however, sleep like the dead. God forbid an alarm go off at night. You could sleep through a hurricane."

Luke smiled, but Rina looked guilty.

"You have slept through a hurricane." Luke threw his head back on the pillow and chuckled.

"Just Gustav!" Rina said defensively. "I was in the closet reading a book. I dozed off and when I woke up, the hurricane was over. Tante D, the traitor, took a video of me. They trot it out whenever they feel I need some added humiliation, like birthdays and holidays. I think you can find it on YouTube." Rina sat on the bed next to him, her chin in her hand and moped.

"Pauvre bête (poor thing)! I can see how that would be traumatic."

Luke rubbed her back. It felt so good, Rina's eyes closed. She was starting to list to the side when she realized Luke was still in her bed. "Leave," she mumbled and then a small moan escaped as Luke went from rubbing to massaging her back.

"Why? Like I said, I've been here every night. When I leave you alone, you have nightmares. I can't let that happen."

"Have not, it was just that one time," Rina murmured.

"Have to, and what are we, twelve?"

Rina yawned as she rolled over. "I'm going to brush my teeth and when I get back, I expect you to be gone." Rina went to one bathroom and Luke to another. When he finished, he undressed and climbed into Rina's bed and turned off the light.

Rina finished her evening ritual, donned her nightgown and climbed into bed. She felt the warm body next to her, the warm body that she was used to, as she drifted off to sleep. She slept deeply as Luke caressed her back.

The next morning Rina woke up snuggled in Luke's arms. She cuddled her head into the crook of his neck, nibbled on his ear and said, "Morning."

Luke's arms tightened around her, and he kissed her temple. "Morning, feelin' frisky?"

Rina waking up a bit more stiffened, "Wait … what?"

"Don't get all defensive. It's just a soft cuddly morning and you are all warm and curvy snuggled up to me and it seemed like the perfect time to make my move."

"Make your move, huh? Alright, Casanova, show me what you got," Rina yawned.

"I would ask you if you were sure, but I don't want you to change your mind." And he swooped down and kissed her. Rina was bracing for a hard, fast kiss. One that scratched the teeth and left lips bruised. Instead, she got nibbles on her full bottom lip and her bow-shaped upper lip. Then he moved to feather light kisses on her eyelids and by her ears. After a nibble on her earlobe, he proceeded nibbling down her jawline to her neck. Rina felt his hands then as they grasped her hips and then squeezed into her waist. She tried not to think about how fat she was. She tried to stay focused, but she squirmed nonetheless.

"What? Is something wrong?"

"Nothing a diet and some willpower couldn't fix."

"Shut up, you're beautiful … lush." With that, he squeezed her waist and then crushed her mouth in an intense kiss. Her legs started kicking out to find some measure. Luke capitalized on that movement to pull Rina's nightgown over her head. His mouth released her as the nightgown flew up. His hands immediately found her breasts. Kneading and then tweaking the nipples before his head dipped down to suckle.

Rina's body bowed, and a moan escaped from her as Luke's hand slid down her stomach, through her curls, until he found her clit. He pinched it lightly as he continued to suckle. Rina braced her hands on the bed and curled her toes in the sheets. As Luke's suckle turned to a nibble Rina bowed up again as a wave of energy started from her feet and shot up through to her hair. She collapsed on the bed, dead to the world.

Luke rested on his elbow, looked down at her and grinned as he kissed her on the temple. Then he rolled out of bed and went down to make coffee. Rina awoke an hour later, a bit discombobulated. She kept trying to tell herself that it was a dream, but her body was thrumming like never before.

Her eyes shot up as Luke came back through the door with two mugs of coffee in his hands. "There you go, sweetheart; gotta keep that energy up. Orgasms can take a lot out of you."

Rina pulled the sheet over her head. "Oh God, that wasn't a dream. Oh, my God. Oh, my God."

"Relax, we're married. We did nothing wrong."

"In name only!" Rina said, swishing the sheet off only to realize she was naked and then tucking it under her arms. The corners of Luke's mouth twitched as he watched Rina. He tried for a blasé air as he set the mugs on the nightstand, but he bobbled one mug at the sight of Rina's breast peaking out from the sheets. He cleared his throat and Rina followed his gaze and quickly righted the sheets.

Luke continued the conversation as if he hadn't just gotten a show. "Well now, after this morning, I would have to disagree with you. I think we very much acted like a married couple. Only it wasn't the man who went to sleep right after the orgasm, leaving the wife high and dry. It was the other way around."

Rina's entire body blushed. At least her face and feet were rosy. "Can we please talk about something else?"

"Sure, how about how we are going to nail Del's ass to the wall?"

"Excellent topic of conversation."

From the doorway Rina heard, "What's an excellent topic of conversation?" Bobby was carrying a tray of food and looking from Luke to Rina.

"Justice," Rina told him diplomatically.

"Bradley says we're going to nail Del's ass to the wall," Bobby parroted.

Luke broke into laughter. "Did he really? Does your mom know?"

"I don't know. Do you think I should tell her?"

"Absolutely!" Luke said.

"You are a disloyal uncle," Rina scolded. "No Bobby, what you should do is tell Mr. Bradley to watch his language around you so that he doesn't get you in trouble."

"Yes, ma'am," Bobby agreed, but he did not look happy. "Oh … here is your breakfast. Mom said you shouldn't have to get up on the day after your wedding to fix breakfast."

Rina looked down at the runny eggs and burned toast. "Ah, thank you, I think?" Rina looked at Luke. "I take it you're the cook in the household?"

"God, yes. Don't eat that. The last time I ate Sarah's cooking was not a good day," Luke warned.

Bobby smiled, "Remember the purple puke, Nonc Luke? Your face was green and your puke was purple. Good thing I ate at Tommy's that night." Rina dropped the toast back on the tray. "Should I throw it in the trash, Nonc Luke? I don't see a compost bin."

"It is out by the fence," Rina informed them.

"Can you sneak it out?" Luke asked.

"Sure thing," Bobby agreed, and he pivoted out the door.

"So Sarah doesn't know she's a terrible cook?" Rina smiled.

"Amazingly oblivious. How she doesn't figure out that toast is not supposed to be black, I don't know."

"Eventually, someone will have to tell her."

"Bradley's problem."

"You're assuming that she will marry Bradley?"

"*Fait accompli* in all but paper. Did you not notice that he is not on the couch when you go make coffee in the morning?"

"I thought he was out walking."

"Nope, he was with Sarah, but she refuses to make an honest man of him. Like me before we got married." Luke tried to give his best leer but failed.

Rina rolled her eyes. "Can we get back to the topic at hand?"

"Sure thing. What was it again?"

"Kicking Del's ass and Porter's too, but I think he is just a pawn of Del. Even when they were tormenting me in my youth, Porter wasn't mean if Del wasn't around. I gave Del the nickname of 'Demon Del' when I was little. I was so happy when they stopped picking on me."

"Yes, that was lucky," Luke said noncommittally.

"So, the plan is to draw them out. They haven't heard about our recent marriage. Del still thinks he can whisk you off to some unscrupulous minister and get you married."

"Do you think he planned on drugging me or something? I mean seriously, how did he think he would get me to say, 'I do'?"

"Good point. You are not a malleable woman."

"Damn straight."

Luke grinned. "Anyway, the plan is to lure them into a trap and catch them before they try to kidnap you."

"Simple enough. How will we do that? I mean, Del will assume after that last attack, we will be on high alert. How do we convincingly let down our guard?"

Luke's cell rang and interrupted their conversation. "Yeah? No shit. We're on our way."

He looked at Rina. "Change of plan. We need to get to the hospital. Someone just bludgeoned Porter on the head."

"I can't. I have to get to school."

"I already called you in sick."

"Excuse me?! I'm not missing school to visit a former bully of mine."

Luke grabbed her hand in his, momentarily distracted by how small and cool it was. "You are now being targeted by someone who has attempted to murder his best friend. Do you think he will be kinder to you? Do you want to bring that target to Meauxville high?"

"*Merde* ... alright, let's go. We can think of a plan to trap Del on the way." Rina grabbed her jacket and Luke's car keys. He opened the door for Rina and then went round to the driver's side and climbed in.

17

As he turned on the car and drove off toward the hospital, he glanced at Rina. Luke flexed his hands on the steering wheel as he tried to compose himself. En route, he looked over at Rina and then he let loose. "I think we should rethink the plan. It is getting too dangerous. You are officially in the hiding portion of the plan, along with Sarah and Bobby."

"What! I am not going to sit around and do nothing while the big, strong men take care of me. Who do you think I am?" Rina fumed.

"Do you really want to risk yourself, Sarah, and Bobby?" Luke asked as they pulled into the hospital parking lot.

"Sarah and Bobby can hide. I have to be in on the plan. I am what Del wants. How do you expect to lure him out of hiding without me?" Rina asked as they got out of the vehicle at the hospital.

Luke hesitated before opening the emergency room doors. "I don't know yet, but we'll think of something."

"Uh huh. Let's just see if Porter is feeling better and feels like giving up his former best friend."

Rina and Luke went to the check-in desk and were greeted by Bradley, who looked grim. "How is he doing? I mean, I'm mad at him for roughing me up, but I don't think he was the brains behind it all."

"No, he just got out of surgery. Del whacked him pretty hard; I didn't think he had that kind of strength in him. I can't believe he nearly killed his best friend. Doctors said Porter should be okay, they are just making sure. We have an APB out on Del and we are searching the area around where Porter was found," Bradley updated them.

"He won't be there. He probably has an underwater lair, the prick," Luke seethed.

Rina smirked, "I always did equate him to Lex Luther, supervillain. He always had a diabolical plot and a backup plan in case things went awry."

"Things are about to go very awry. Where are Sarah and Bobby?" Luke fumed.

"I had them picked up as soon as we found Porter. I know that they would be perfect leverage for Del. Do you think we should just let him know that it is over and that you are married?"

"What! And give up our biggest lure to catch him? I don't think so. As long as Rina, Sarah, and Bobby are safe, we go ahead with our plan."

Bradley looked stymied. "But if Rina is safe, how are we going to lure Del out of the woodwork?"

"Exactly my point." Rina interjected.

Luke ignored her comment and continued, "So what we need to do is to make Del believe Rina will be somewhere, unprotected. Then he will try to nab her and we can get him."

"Brilliant plan," Rina said. "Simple and concise, but there is one problem. How will you be able to convince Del that I am doing something when I'm locked up in some safe house?"

"She has a point, Luke." Bradley agreed, "Sarah and Bobby need to be safe because they could be pawns, but we need Rina."

"Would you let Sarah do it?" Luke asked him.

"Hell, no! But then again, she would probably insist and come up with her own scheme with the help of Rina. Then those two would put that scheme into action without my knowledge or protection ... so maybe. I guess I could just tie her up."

"Bobby would untie her." Rina smirked.

"Not if I gave him chocolate and allowed him to play 'Call of Duty' until he untied his momma."

Rina laughed, "It would probably work. Particularly if you tell him it is to protect his mom. However, you do not have that option with me."

"I could tie you up," Luke piped in. His brain digressing off on all kinds of salacious tangents.

"Yes, but Sarah would untie me and neither of you hold sway over Sarah."

"Fine, fine. You are in the plan, but you do what we say when we say it."

"Don't I always?" Rina said, looking at him angelically. Luke snorted and then started as he saw a doctor walking towards them.

"Lt. Bradley?"

"Yes, that's me."

"I'm Dr. Johnson, Mr. Douguet's attending physician. I wanted to let you know your prisoner is stable. There is no more brain swelling, and he appears to be recovering nicely."

"When can I speak with him?" Bradley asked.

"I would say in a couple of hours. He needs to rest a bit, but if all goes well, he should be able to speak to you soon."

"Understood. I have a guard on his door. Your staff will need to show their ID to get in to see him."

"Is that really necessary?" the doctor asked, perturbed that his staff would be subjected to that kind of treatment.

"Doctor, the man who attempted to murder him and twice attempted to kidnap Ms. LeBlanc is still on the loose, and his brutal behavior is escalating. I will have an officer on patrol in the hospital, as well, to make sure you are all safe."

Comprehending the truth of Bradley's statement, Dr. Johnson thanked him and took his leave.

"Okay, so what is the plan?" Rina asked, running her hands through her curls.

Luke thought about it, and as he thought, his arm slid around Rina's waist. "We need a time when Del thinks that you are alone. Why would you even be alone based on what has already happened?"

"If I wanted to think?" Rina suggested. "Del used to spend most of his time tormenting me. He knows that when I'm upset or confused, I like to be alone to sort things out. God knows he found and tormented me often enough in my youth to have discerned that pattern."

Luke's hold tightened a bit. "I'm going to kill that rodent."

"Officer of the law here," Bradley reminded them. "Hold your tongue. You can't say shit like that when I'm within earshot."

"*Je vas le tuer, cette espèce de rat,*" Luke revised in French.

"Well, okay then, that is above my level of French and thus gives me plausible deniability. Also, judges hate trying to figure out what we say in French, anyway. However, it still does not resolve your problem. You need a plan."

They mulled over various ideas on the drive to *Chêne Vert*. Once they arrived, they sat at the kitchen table discussing and rejecting ideas. They couldn't figure a way to convince Del that Rina wasn't just being used to bait a trap.

"Why don't you pretend to fight?" came another voice from the doorway.

"Why are you always interjecting comments from doorways, Bobby?" Rina asked. "It is a good idea, though."

Bobby smiled, "I know, I'm gifted. One day, I will be a gifted alchemist."

Sarah came up behind him and put her hand on his shoulder. "I knew I should have never had him tested."

"What are you doing here?! You are supposed to be in a safe house. Where the hell is Richard?" Bradley questioned.

"We gave him the slip," Bobby chortled.

"It is not funny!" Bradley yelled. "You two are not safe! Del nearly killed a man, and he knows how much you both mean to Rina! He could kidnap you and use you as leverage!"

"Okay, okay. Stop yelling. I just figured we would be as safe with you as with Sgt. Richard," Sarah said, trying to calm Bradley down while keeping a reassuring hand on Bobby.

"Great, that's great, so instead of being able to give my full attention to protecting your best friend, Rina, I will split my attention between you, Bobby and Rina. That's just great."

"Alright already, we'll go back." Sarah turned for the door.

"You are not going anywhere by yourselves until Del is behind bars or dead."

He angled his head to speak into his shoulder-communication device — "Richard, are you there, you loser? I have your wards over here. Apparently, they wandered off while you were examining your toenails."

"Sarah asked me for help to find a suitcase and she locked me in the closet. I just got out."

"Jesus Christ, Sarah."

"I just wanted to see you, Bradley."

"Sarah, I need you safe. Do you understand? I need to know that you and Bobby are safe for me to function at all."

"Fine, I'll go back with Sgt. Richard, but you call me. You keep me informed of what is going on."

"I will text, but don't text me. I can't have my phone vibrating at a crucial time."

Rina, Luke, and Bobby were watching the play-by-play. Rina looked at Luke and said, "You're right. It is like they are already married."

"No," Bobby responded, "Then I could call Mr. Bradley 'Dad', and I can't do that, at least not yet."

Sarah started at the unadulterated longing in Bobby's voice. "We have to go now, baby," she told him. "Tell Nonc Luke and Tante Rina your plan."

"Well, what you need to do is pretend that you are really close. Do that gross kissy stuff and go out to eat and all that other gushy stuff. Then, somewhere very public, you need to get into a fight. Tante Rina will stomp off in a huff, you know, like Mommy when she is losing an argument, but outside to like a dark alley. Then Nonc Luke needs to stomp to his car and drive off. It would be the perfect time to snatch Tante Rina."

Luke, Bradley, and Rina looked at Bobby, astounded. "That is a fabulous idea." Luke told him.

"Told you I'm gifted," Bobby gloated.

"Yes," Rina smiled, "I can see that you are. So, first I get courted and then I get to have a knock-down drag-out fight in public. Except for the crazed, murderous villain, that actually sounds like fun."

Bobby was glowing when he and Sarah left under the careful, if annoyed, guard of Sgt. Richard.

"Great, so where are you taking me for a romantic dinner, Luke? I'm thinking that I want some shrimp *étouffée* or a catfish *courtbouillon*. What about some boiled shrimp?"

"You really think peeling shrimp is romantic?"

"If you peel them all for me, it is."

"We can go eat at Café Prudhomme's. Enola is feeling better and you love the bread."

"Umm jalapeno bread with honey butter. She has to-die-for crawfish enchiladas. Oh, can we go now?"

"No, she doesn't open until 5 pm. Besides, you need to get home and gussy yourself up for me. I prefer a dress and the color green."

"As if."

"We are pretending to be courting, so you need to pretend to want to impress me."

"Fine, fine. I will wear my prettiest dress and knock your socks off. When do we get to do our free-for-all fight?"

"Not for a while. We need Del to worry that he is losing out, and then have you break up with me."

"Can I slap you? I'm fantastic at that! I think you should let me slap you to prove how angry I am with you."

"No, you can't assault me. Save that rage for Del, I'm innocent here."

"Oh alright, you wimp. Have it your way. Let's go back home and prepare for our first scene."

"Remember when I said you had no talent for acting? I take it back. Were you a chemistry major with a theater minor, by chance?" Luke asked as he opened to the door for Rina.

"Nope, just a thespian wannabe," Rina joked when they got to Luke's truck. Luke unlocked the door and smiled.

18

After dinner, since Sarah and Bobby were at a safe house, Rina and Luke checked all the locks, turned on the new security system (rapidly installed thanks to Bradley's contacts), and climbed the stairs to her room.

"You know, you can go to your own room. It is not like anyone would notice that we are not sleeping in the same bed. Besides, everyone we know knows that you married me just to keep me safe."

"Not true." Luke responded.

"What's not true?"

"All of what you said. One, I can't go to my room because I couldn't sleep if you are alone and unprotected. Cave man of me, I know, but the truth, nonetheless. In addition, it's clear you can't sleep without me, either. You get nightmares and I end up sleeping in here, anyway. Whether you believe it or not, it is where I have slept for the past three weeks. Finally, everyone we know knows that I married you because I wanted to marry you and finally saw my chance and took it."

"You are certifiable."

"Most likely," and he went to take a shower in the *en suite* bathroom.

Rina resisted a smile as she reviewed her sub's lesson plans. She had been trying to keep them as simple as possible. The kids must be bored out of their minds, she thought. At least she was sending them good stories to read. Zosimus and his four elements (air, water, wind, and fire). She'll tell stories about his work and the fact that some of it was lost when the Christians burned the library at Alexandria. Well, the daughter library anyway. Still a great story. Rina smiled.

"What is so funny?" Luke asked. Rina looked up but was temporarily stunned to see Luke in nothing but a towel. She opened her mouth to respond, but nothing came out. It just sort of hung open until she noticed and abruptly shut it. Even then, her mouth had gotten so dry that she had to swallow and lick her lips. Although she wasn't sure if the lip licking was due to the dry mouth or the sight of Luke in nothing but his towel. Wait, he had asked her a question. What was the question again? She tried to think, but couldn't remember. "I'm sorry. What did you say?"

Luke grinned that cat-with-the-cream-pot grin and asked her again in an exaggeratedly slow voice. "What ... is ... so ... funny? You were smiling when I came in."

"That the Christians burned down the library."

"Our library? I didn't hear about a fire, and why would that be funny?"

Rina laughed. "Not our library. Over 1,600 years ago in Alexandria, 391 AD, to be exact. They burned down part of the great Alexandrian Library, which housed all the knowledge of the world and set us back centuries."

"Oh ... and we are talking about this, why?"

"Because it is one of the stories that my sub is telling the students while I'm away. I figured since I wasn't going to trust a sub with experiments with volatile chemicals, then I could at least make her a storyteller and let her tell all the stories that I don't have time to tell."

"Only you would make chemistry read-aloud time." Luke smiled and lay on the bed in his towel.

Rina lost her breath. "Umm ... aren't you going to change into your PJs?"

"Sure, but I was thinking of doing that once you left the room to take your shower. But if you would rather I change now..." Luke reached to unwrap his towel.

"No! I mean, no, that's okay. I'll just go ... now. I'll just go now and take ... my shower. So here I am going ... to take my shower." Rina tripped over her words and then nearly tripped over her vanity bench, running to the bathroom.

Once she got inside, she slammed the door and just leaned on it, trying to catch her breath. She looked in the mirror. Her face was beet red beneath her unruly curls. "Smooth Rina, real smooth." She banged her head against the door a couple of times in penance.

"You okay in there?" Luke called out.

"Kill me now," she whispered, and then thought of Del and took it back. "Just fine. Just getting into my shower."

"You might try turning on the water first," Luke called through the door.

"Already on it," Rina said, as she went to turn on her shower so she could wash away the humiliation.

Luke relaxed on the bed and looked around Rina's room. He had been truthful when he said that he had been sleeping in her room for the past three weeks, but he really hadn't gotten a chance to take a closer look. Even yesterday, waking with Rina for the first time, instead of sneaking off before dawn, he was too busy arguing and doing other things with her to notice the space.

The white brass bed with a blue-colored comforter. What did she call it? 'Bog sage blue'. An old wooden bench and vanity with an old silver brush and mirror on it. Luke knew that Rina never used the brush. He had seen Rina brush her hair once, and it turned into a comical mass of frizz around her head. Luke smiled at the memory.

Next to the vanity was her bookshelf, a mix of chemistry treatises, romance novels, and pop-artist biographies. Luke once asked her why she liked reading about the lives of pop artists. Rina beamed and said that it was because they were just so damn mediocre. When she read biographies of great people, she just felt small and insignificant, but when she read about, say, New Kids on the Block, their Boston roots, and how they practiced after school, she felt like mediocre greatness might be within her reach.

Luke shook his head at the memory and listened as the water shut off. Before Rina got out of the bathroom, he flung off his towel and installed himself on the bed. He climbed under the covers, but his chest remained naked as he grabbed a book randomly off Rina's shelf. Great, a romance novel! But he started reading anyway and was actually enjoying the antics of the blond bombshell who vacationed at a golf resort and then proceeded to injure and maim her suitors.

Rina walked in and smiled, "*Manhunting*. I love that book."

"This woman is crazy!"

"Where are you in the book?" Rina asked as she took off the towel turban and dried her hair with it.

"She just jabbed a suitor for trying to take her mashed potatoes."

"Mashed potatoes are important. Particularly homemade mashed potatoes." Rina folded the towel and hung it to dry inside the bathroom.

"She drew blood."

"Yes, but she did not get the blood on her mashed potatoes. You are missing the important parts." Rina chuckled, returning to the room and then her laughter faded as she noticed that Luke's chest was bare and that he was already tucked underneath the covers, her covers. Luke patted the bed and his eyes gleamed.

"No fooling around," Rina said.

"I would never fool around. I'm serious; you need to lie down. You're looking peaked. Why don't you lie down and I'll rub your back?"

"I don't think that is a good idea," Rina said and climbed into bed in her bathrobe.

"Are you sleeping with that thing on?" Luke asked.

"I think it would be more appropriate."

"What it will be is uncomfortable. C'mon Rina, it is not like I'm going to ravish you. If I do anything that bothers you, just say 'No' and it stops immediately."

"Promise?"

"Scout's honor." And he put his finger up in what he thought looked like a Scout-ish manner.

"Luke Hebert, you never have been or never will be a Boy Scout, so don't even try that on me."

"Fine Rina, but I give you my word. I will do nothing that you don't want me to do."

"Was that a double negative?"

"Good God, woman, negotiating with a teacher is a pain in the ass. If you say 'No', I stop, word of honor. Clear enough?"

Rina relaxed then. She turned off the side lamp, removed her bathrobe, and snuggled under the covers. Much to Luke's dismay, she had a nightgown underneath the robe. She wriggled around several times, trying to find a comfortable position, but she was too worked up today.

"Luke?"

"Yes Rina?"

"My back really does hurt. My neck too. Can you rub them for me?"

"Sure. Turn over."

Rina flopped over on her stomach. Luke rubbed his hands together to warm them and then gently began massaging Rina's back. Her deep breathing was bad enough, but when he reached her neck, she started emitting little moans of pleasure. Luke closed his eyes and tried to resist, but since she had let him do a little something yesterday, he wondered what he could get away with. The next pass on her back, he slid his hands over the side of her torso, gently brushing past the side of her breasts.

Then his hands went lower, down her back, down to her rounded ass. His hands cupped it and squeezed, and Rina let out another moan. He moved back up, massaging as he went. Following the lines of her ribs from her back to her chest. Until he was skimming her breasts again, only this time, he held them, tweaking the nipples between his fingers and lightly skimming the roundness of them with his fingertips before he reached around and cupped them as he pressed hot, wet kisses onto Rina's back.

Rina arched her back and moaned. Turning her head, she succumbed to Luke's kisses, biting his lower lip, and pulling him against her as she turned over. Rina's hands flew over his back, down to his firm rear and then around to wrap her fingers around him as he moaned.

Luke began nipping at her jaw, nibbling on her ear, and then down her throat. He sucked on her breast through the thin cotton fabric of her nightgown. Using his tongue to roll her nipple under his upper teeth. And then his hands gripped her hips, as he slowly kissed his way down her body. Licking at her belly button until the fabric was soaked, he lifted her gown up as he bit and nipped at Rina's inner thigh.

Wedging his shoulders between her legs, steading her hips with his hands, Luke began to lick into her, at first just random licks and then more concentrated. He let her shudders guide him to discover what she liked. Finding her clit with his tongue, Luke nipped and sucked, sending waves of ecstasy through

Rina. As one hand left her hip and slid to her core, he sent one finger inside her while he continued sucking and rolling her clit over his teeth. Her nerves ratcheted up another level when he put another finger inside her. The hand on her hip caressed her ass, taking her to even higher.

She couldn't escape the wracking sensations. In the front was Luke's mouth on her, his fingers in her. In the back, Luke's hand squeezing her ass with one finger slipping between her cheeks, that naughty finger. The sensations grew and grew. The sucking, biting, and pressure until Rina broke in a scream. Her hips pistoned as her fingers threaded through Luke's hair, keeping his mouth locked on her clit.

And then there was nothing but a floaty darkness. She awoke to Luke's soft snores as he spooned around her. She cuddled closer and fell asleep with him.

19

Del was not doing well. He paced the floor of the dive hotel room he had for the night. The whore he had hired had fled, and he had a feeling he did not have much more time before her pimp came in and made him pay for the damaged goods. He probably should not have tried to get someone who looked like Rina.

When she was his, he would make her pay. But apparently she was taking up with Luke Hebert. A nobody, a grease monkey who always seemed to be around to throw a wrench in his plans. Worse, he knew that Luke, while being nobody, was still related to the town's founding fathers and thus would be eligible for Rina's dowry if he got it in his mind to marry Rina. "So I will just have to keep that from happening."

Del grabbed his gun and started out the door. He was going to have to do some surveillance before he tried anything, which meant he needed a place to hide. Walking in Rina's neighborhood at night, he noticed the tree house and decided it was the best place to monitor Rina. However, he also saw Luke's truck parked in Rina's driveway **at three in the morning**. Del fumed.

'Not a problem,' Del thought to himself. It will only be a couple of days, and then Rina and her dowry would be his. He didn't care if Rina slept around, as long as her money stayed with him. He climbed the ladder up to the tree house and went to sleep.

The next morning Rina woke up with her legs intertwined with Luke's. She felt a hard ridge against her stomach. She leaned into Luke, pressing his member into her soft belly. Luke woke with a groan and dug his fingers into her waist and grabbed her to pull her tighter against him.

Rina nibbled on his neck, brushed her face against the soft curly hair on his chest, and angled her legs so that the hard shaft was between her thighs. She closed her legs together then, locking her ankles and moving back and forth, feeling him brush against her increasing wetness.

Luke was fully awake by then. Grabbing her hips and he adjusted her so that he could enter her with one slow, long pulse. He pulled out nearly to the entrance and pulsed back in. He continued doing that very methodically, out until he was almost free of her and back in until she could feel him in her womb. As he pulsed, his hands held her breasts and tweaked her nipples. He bit the back of her neck.

As she tightened around him, one of Luke's hands eased down Rina's body. His fingers found her clit. He pinched it lightly between his thumb and forefinger as he rubbed her nipple with his other hand. At the same time, he had taken to biting and licking Rina's ear. Through it all was the slow pulse, in all the way, out nearly all the way, in again. Rina shook her head.

"Yes," Luke said, "fight it. You don't want to come for me. You can keep it away. Don't you come, Rina," he said, as he pinched and flicked and licked. "Be a good girl, Rina. This is not what you are supposed to be doing? You are being very naughty." Luke's low, deep voice chuckled as he was in and out and nibbling everywhere.

"Very naughty Rina. Naughty Rina, you should not be liking this." He increased his pace. "I think you should be spanked. That's how naughty you are."

Rina moaned at the thought.

"Waking me up and taking me without a by-your-leave. Seducing me while I slept," as the hand on her breast gave a final tweak to her nipple before it came down on her shapely bum with a slap. Rina moaned and her hips jerked violently against Luke. "Definitely, you should not come. I will have to punish you if you come, Rina. You don't want me to punish you now, do you?" A slap on her ass reverberated through her, as he pumped and tweaked and licked and groaned, and Rina came.

Spiraling out of control, her body bowed, her sheath throbbing around him, until he, too, let loose a shout and poured into her. Exhausted, they lay in each other's arms, unable to move, unable to think.

Rina drifted off immediately, as Luke had already learned she was wont to do. Luke pulled away from her, rubbing his hands up and down her body, admiring the handprints on her buttocks and knowing that she was his. He fell asleep wrapped around her, his hands cupping her breasts.

Rina woke up feeling a little sore. She went to move and noticed Luke behind her and Luke's hands in front of her. She grinned. 'OMG,' she thought.

She moved to get up and Luke's hands tightened on her breasts, sending a bolt of 'yum' through her system. She had to get up, though. Nature was calling. She tried to pry Luke's hands off her. Instead, they tightened, and then he rolled her nipples between his thumb and forefinger. She felt his smile against her hair.

"Let me up! I have to pee!"

"Fine," Luke said, "ruin my fun." But he let her get up and admired the view as she streaked into the bathroom. When Rina came out, she had a serious look on her face. "Ah Luke, I think we forgot something."

"What?"

"Protection."

"We have a cop outside. The doors are locked, and the alarm system is armed. I think we are pretty protected, Rina."

Rina laughed. "I don't think Richard or the alarm are going to keep me from getting pregnant. And the doors would have only worked if you were on the other side of them."

"Oh," Luke said, as sudden understanding struck.

Rina laughed again, "Yes, oh."

"Well, it was only that one time, and I will keep condoms around for the future."

"For the future. You think we'll be doing this again?"

Luke's eyes smoldered. "We'll definitely be doing that again. Numerous times in numerous places. In fact, I'm stocking condoms in every room in the house and in the tree house, just in case."

Rina blushed and tried to change the subject. She hesitated. "Coffee ... we need coffee and breakfast. I'm starving. Can we go out for breakfast? That is my favorite meal to eat out."

"Absolutely, besides I have to start courting you, and a breakfast out is the perfect way to start."

20

Rina and Luke dressed, locked and armed the house, and then jumped into the truck. Del noticed that Luc's hand rested possessively on Rina's back as he escorted her to the truck. 'Great,' he thought, 'they **are** doing it. Well, eight million dollars was worth sloppy seconds.'

Del climbed down when the truck was out of sight and went to go snoop in the house. Unfortunately for him, he did not see the alarm signs because they were on the front of the house. As he forced open the back doors, an alarm started screaming, and lights started flashing. Del hesitated, stunned. Then he heard the sheriff's sirens.

He ran out of the house and up to the tree house. Since Meauxville did not have a K9 unit to find his scent, he figured staying close by was a better option than fleeing to God knows where again.

Bradley was just finishing up the morning dishes when he got the text. He looked up at Sarah. "Break in at Rina's place. The perp fled. I need to go."

"Can we go, too?" Sarah asked.

Bradley's instinctual response was a resounding "NO!" but there were already officers at the scene, and Sarah should be pretty safe. Del was already long gone. "Fine, but you...."

"Do what you say when you say it," Sarah and Bobby chimed together.

Bradley smiled, mussed Bobby's hair, and said, "exactly."

Luke and Rina had just gotten to the restaurant when his cell phone rang. "Yeah?" he asked. Luke listened for a minute and then said, "We'll be right there."

He got up, and Rina asked. "What's wrong?"

"Break in at your house. Now tell me, 'you were right, Luke, I needed an alarm system'."

"You were right, Luke. Is he still there?" As she said it, she pulled backwards against Luke's arm as though she was instinctually trying to avoid that situation.

Luke once again promised himself that he would ring Del's neck. "No, he fled the scene. C'mon."

They left the diner and headed back to *Chêne Vert*. When they got to the house, it was mayhem, with cops everywhere. Rina saw Sarah and Bobby and went to greet them. "Y'all okay?" Rina asked.

"Fine, just trying to figure out what happened. We can't go and ask, because we both promised to behave, and Bradley's last words to us were 'stay put'."

"Well, I'll keep you company. Bradley!" Rina shouted when she caught sight of him. "Did anyone see anything?"

"No, Mrs. Robichaux said that y'all's dog, Stewart, was going nuts just before she heard the alarms. In fact, he is still going nuts, and she had to leash him to keep him in place," Bradley said.

Rina froze at his statement. "That means Del's still around."

"No, he is long gone. There's no way we would have missed him if he were still around."

Rina shook her head. "Stewart would know. That dog can find anything with his nose. I walk him every day, I should know. Let him look. He's somewhere, Bradley. I can feel him watching me."

"Rina, I really think ..." Bradley started.

"What would it hurt if you let the dog out?" Sarah asked, putting her arm around Rina.

"It's impossible to win with you two," Bradley stated.

"And yet you keep trying," Sarah retorted. "Let's get Stewart."

As they walked over to convince Mrs. Robichaux to let them take the agitated Stewart for another walk, Del was watching them through binoculars. His new abode was well outfitted with blankets, food, and binoculars.

However, he saw his nice cozy situation deteriorate as Rina went over to the next-door neighbor to collect her crazed dog. Del considered shooting the animal, but decided that retreat was his best option.

He grabbed the binoculars, his gun, and a bag of chips, and climbed down the ladder before they could bring the dog around to the back of the house. Just as he made it through the shrubbery, he heard the dog coming after him.

He hightailed it through the woods to the bayou, hoping that the film myth that a dog would lose a trail if you crossed water was accurate. Brambles and branches tore at his clothes. As he escaped, his rage at the injustice and rotten luck he was having irked him. Nothing was working out. Now he was stuck in the woods with no money, no place to stay, and nothing but a bag of chips to eat.

They saw the ladder of the tree house swinging as Stewart dragged Rina to the backyard. Bradley nodded to Richard to clear the tree house while he continued to stick by Rina as she let Stewart drag her into the woods. He was barking non-stop and hot on the trail of whoever had broken into her house—Del, Rina figured.

He had been in the tree house ... in her tree house ... in Sarah's tree house...in Bobby's tree house. Rina was livid. Her face turned red, and her hold on the leash tightened as she raced behind Stewart. She was going to kill Del. She had had enough.

Luke had to sprint to keep up with her. "I didn't realize that you were in such good shape." His breath ragged, he asked, "when did you take up running again?"

"I didn't," Rina exclaimed, "This is just pure, unadulterated rage."

When they got to the bayou, Stewart stopped barking, and he stopped running. Luke put his hands on his knees to catch his breath while Rina scanned for any sign of Del. Bradley phoned in their location so they could try to catch him on his way out of the woods. Then they walked back to the house.

"He's gone. We had him, and now he is gone!" Exhausted, Rina started to wobble. Luke caught her, and she swung her arms in rage, screaming. Sarah hugged Bobby to her as they watched Rina implode. Tears streamed down her face as she struggled against Luke's hold. Then she just sank to the ground, holding her knees.

"I'm so tired of this!" she moaned. Luke picked Rina up and held her as she cried.

"I think we need to take a little break," he said as he kissed her temple and carried her inside.

"You're probably right. We were going too fast. We got caught up in the whole living together and marriage thing."

"What?"

"You probably want to move out. I'll go to the safe house with Sarah and Bobby."

"What are you talking about? I didn't mean us. We are finally where we should be. I just think that you need an evening where you don't have to think about Del." He set her lightly on the living room couch.

"That sounds wonderful, but highly unlikely. His essence is pervasive. I don't think there is an anti-Del Febreze or anything. Although, that would be a great invention. If only one could buy a product that could clear one's head of thoughts of someone."

"There is such a product. It is called fun. Come with me to the fair." He sat beside her and pulled her feet on to his lap.

"You mean the place that sells questionable food using questionable sanitary practices and then offers death defying rides that are monitored and constructed by carnies who have little to no engineering background?" She leaned back as they spoke and let him rub her feet.

"Well, that is what I had thought, but your take on it doesn't seem as fun as I had anticipated."

"We should all go bowling," Sarah said, joining them.

"I did miss bowling with you the night...."

"Shhhht..." Luke put his finger over her lips. "No discussing he-who-cannot-be-named."

"Like Voldemort?" Bobby asked.

"Yes, like 'Flight of death'," Rina said.

At Bobby's quizzical look, she explained that's what Voldemort meant in French.

"See," Bradley said to Sarah, "This is why you should let me teach Bobby French. Look at all he learns."

"Except that with you, all he will learn is how to curse in French."

"An important skill," Luke interjected.

Sarah shot a look at Luke. "Don't think I forgot that you already taught him some choice words. I can tell what he says when he is muttering."

Rina smiled because that is what they were trying to get her to do, but she still felt hunted.

21

Twenty minutes later, they all had their bowling shoes on and Luke and Bradley were ordering beer, a cola for Bobby, and pizza.

"This is great!" Bobby said.

"Yes, it is." Sarah responded, "Rina, can you guard my lucky ball? Somebody keeps trying to hide it and somebody else," she darted her accusative eyes at Bobby, "is a useless guard when bribed by chocolate." Bobby tried to look innocent.

Sarah went to go make sure that they were ordering at least one vegetarian pizza. Rina decided to make small talk. "So Bobby, how is school?"

"I haven't been to school since we moved to the boring house."

"Boring house?"

"Yes, I want my treehouse back."

"Already claimed it, have you? I have always thought of it as your mom's treehouse."

"Yes, but she bequeathed it to me."

"Don't you have to be dead to bequeath something?"

"She bequeathed it proactively."

"Are you kidding me?"

"Yes, but I still get the treehouse."

"You got it." Rina smiled and relaxed into the conversation. "What have you been learning about lately?"

"Well, I learned about the first nonfictitious alchemist. Maria the Jewess or Prophetissa. She was a Syrian princess who studied under Aristotle. She created the still."

"And Tante Rina perfected it," Luke said, overhearing the last of the conversation.

"What's a still for?" Bobby asked.

"It is a way to use heat, liquids, and certain metals like copper to create chemical reactions," Rina said.

"Like Scotch," Bradley said. "Excellent invention."

"Okay, let's bowl!" Sarah said as she came back, and they did.

"**W**oo-hoo," Sarah flung her hands up and skipped out to the parking lot. "Geez, woman, control yourself," Bradley grunted, a bit put out.

"I'm sorry, I'm just happy. It is a beautiful night," Sarah said with a tipsy grin.

"How does she bowl better when she drinks?" Bradley asked Luke.

"I don't know. That is why I told you to stop offering her beer."

"I thought it would give us the advantage," Bradley said. Rina and Bobby laughed.

"You," Sarah slurred, "You are a cheat, and that is why, that is why," she said as she stepped closer to Bradley. "That is why...." Sarah's voice went astray as she leaned in close to poke Bradley in the chest. She stared into his eyes and froze. Then she blinked. "What was I trying to say?" Sarah asked him.

Bradley was stunned silent, staring at Sarah's mouth.

"That is why," Bobby interjected helpfully.

"Yesss," Sarah slurred, "that is why you lost and I won."

"What is why?" Rina asked teasingly.

"What is what?" Sarah asked.

"That's what I'd like to know," Luke said *sotto voce* to Rina. She snickered.

"Now, what was I saying?" Sarah asked the party at large.

"Bobby, I have a word for you. *Saoule* ... it's pronounced like *sous*, as in under, with an 'l' on the end." Bradley stated, trying to hold Sarah up when she slipped while admiring the stars.

"*Saoule*," Bobby repeated. "What does it mean?"

"Drunk as a skunk." Luke said. "Let's try this phrase, *Maman est saoule.*"

"Don't you teach him that!" Sarah slurred, affronted.

"*Maman est saoule. Maman est très saoule*," Bobby said, improvising.

"*Très bien*," Bradley and Luke said simultaneously.

"No, no, Rina, you have to help me out here. No one taught me French, except a few curse words," Sarah pleaded.

"Fine," Rina acquiesced. "Bobby, try this one. Point to Bradley and say, *Tu es canaille.*"

"Rina! I'm shocked," Bradley said.

"That's right, Bradley! You're sneaky." Sarah agreed, poking her finger into his chest with each word.

"*Tu es canaille,* Mr. Bradley," Bobby said, enjoying his impromptu French lesson. This was nothing like Mme. Savoy's class. You only learned colors, numbers, and stupid songs in her class. "Now this is French I can use," Bobby added. "*Tu es canaille aussi, Nonc Luke.*"

"So if Bradley and Nonc Luke are *canaille* and Mom is *saoule*, what is Tante Rina?" Bobby asked.

"*Smatte*," Rina said, and winked at him.

They parted ways in the middle of the lot, with Sarah, Bradley and Bobby going to his patrol car, and Luke and Rina heading to Luke's truck. When they got back to *Chêne Vert*, Rina was nervous. "What if he went inside?" she asked.

"That's doubtful. The alarms scared him right away, and he was in the treehouse nearby, so there was no reason to enter the house. C'mon, let's get you inside champ."

Rina smiled. "We did win, didn't we? Sarah is a hawk when she's wasted."

"I know. She is the only person I know whose reaction times and coordination improve as she gets more and more buzzed. It is astonishing and annoying at the same time."

"It is only annoying if you are not on her team. When she is playing with you, it is a wondrous sight to see," Rina teased.

After getting inside and locking the doors, Rina and Luke headed to bed. This time there was no demurring. Rina changed into her nightgown without batting an eye, brushed her teeth, and crashed on the bed.

'Great,' Luke thought, 'from strangers to newlyweds to an old married couple in three days flat.' Rina was already asleep when he climbed in to bed. As he adjusted the covers, she rolled over to him, snuggled her head in the crook of his shoulder, and put her hand on his chest. She also did the funniest thing with her feet. She slid her feet so that his Achille's tendon was between her two first toes. It was an oddly possessive position. A Rinaesque claim that charmed him. He hugged her closer and then fell asleep.

B loody, muddy, and enraged, Del had had enough. He was not going to run anymore. 'Think,' he told himself, 'what is the use of superior intellect if panic supersedes my brain processes? The thing about a superior intellect,' he thought, 'was that geniuses tend to make fewer mistakes than the masses.' So that was his new plan. He simply had to wait for the simpletons to make a mistake. Of course they would. They were idiots. Lucky idiots, he would concede, but idiots, nonetheless. Perhaps he could augment the pressure on them, with some accidents strictly *casu consulto* (accidentally on purpose). People invariably make more mistakes when they are under a lot of pressure. Del circled back towards *Chêne Vert.*

Luke woke up and snuggled closer to Rina. He heard Stewart going crazy next door, right before he smelled the smoke. "Rina," he shook her, "Rina sweetie, get up, there is a fire."

Luke grabbed his phone and called 911 as he and Rina rushed out of the house. They were nearly out the front door when his instincts kicked in. "Wait!" he said, pulling on Rina's arm.

"What, we need to get out of here," Rina said, pulling back.

"We are being smoked out. We need to leave by a different door ... out the garage."

Rina and Luke crawled to the kitchen door to go out through the garage. Once in the garage, they climbed into Luke's truck and opened the garage door automatically. Luke was backing out when Del shot out his back window.

"Get down!" he screamed to Rina and then slammed on the accelerator.

Del got off another shot before he had to run to avoid getting crushed by Luke's truck. The shot went wild as Luke's truck barreled towards him.

He heard the sirens of the fire truck and the sheriff coming closer as he made his escape.

$$\text{22}$$

"Okay," Luke said, "It looks like all is well. He must have just tried to smoke us out. I don't see any flames." Luke looked over, but Rina was still on the floor. She was still crouched there, unmoving. "Rina?" Luke said, "Are you okay?" Rina did not respond, but he heard a whimper. "Rina, are you okay?"

"No," Rina's voice was shaky.

"Where! Rina! Where were you hit?"

"My arm, it hurts. Can't talk."

"I got you, baby. Let me find the ambulance." Luke drove towards the sirens and flashed down the ambulance. The bullet had pierced Rina's upper arm. According to the EMT, the wound was non-life threatening, but there was a lot of blood loss. Rina's face looked pale as the medic worked on her. He suggested that she go to the hospital to ensure that all was well. "You might need some blood," the medic said.

"Can I go tomorrow? I just want to go see how *Chêne Vert* is. Tante Dianne left me to care for the house and now Del has tried to burn it down."

"I don't think there is much damage, Rina. I think it was mostly smoke."

Once the medic had finished with Rina, she stood, and wobbled, and then fell against Luke. "Hospital." Luke said.

"Not yet. I need to check on the house. I won't be able to relax until I know *Chene Vert* is alright."

"Fine, but then we go to the hospital. You get some blood, and then we go meet Sarah and Bobby at the safe house."

"No! I don't want to chance that Del follows, and then Sarah and Bobby will get caught in the crossfire."

"Fine, let's go back and check on *Chêne Vert,* and then we will play it by ear."

Anxious, Rina moved to rush out of the car as soon as she saw *Chêne Vert*. Luke grabbed her hand. "Let's wait for the all clear from Bradley."

Bradley was walking towards them. "You okay?"

"Rina got hit, but she refuses to go to the hospital until she sees that the house is okay."

Bradley shook his head in obvious disapproval. "Can't you control your woman, Luke? It's pathetic."

Bradley shot Rina a smile. "The house is fine. Del tried to start a fire using your chopped firewood, but apparently his brilliant mind did not understand that when wood that is stored outside in Louisiana, it tends to be very wet. Plus, you stacked it next to your cistern. So even though he used accelerants to get the first sparks going, as soon as the cistern caught on fire, all that stored rainwater simply put the fire out."

"How much damage to the Cistern?" Rina asked, trying to crane her head around them both and see the damage.

"Should take a few slats of wood. No problem. I'm setting a full-time watch on you and your house. So when you are here, there will be two deputies watching you, and when you leave, you will always have a tail."

Rina was about to argue that it wasn't necessary, but decided that perhaps arson, trespassing and two counts of attempted kidnapping, and a shooting warranted that kind of protection.

Rina walked with Luke to go and look at the damage. It really wasn't bad. "I'll call to get it fixed today."

Luke could see Rina calculating in her head. "I can help pay for it if you need it," Luke said.

"No, no, it just means that it might be awhile before I can pay all the ransom on my car," Rina smiled at him.

Luke smiled back. Apparently, she had already forgotten about her windfall and that she was a millionaire.

They turned back to the truck. En route, she started to sway. "Okay, next stop doctorland," Luke said, and swung her up to carry her the rest of the way.

"I'm fine!" Rina insisted. "I just tripped."

"Un huh. Close your eyes and touch your nose."

"I'm not drunk!" Rina said, "I'm just a little tired."

"Really?" Luke set her down and stepped back. Rina took one step, and then her world began to spin. Luke caught her back up. "You were saying?" he said smugly.

"Can we skip over the 'I told you so's'?"

"As long as they are implied, I am fine with that." Rina slumped against Luke in the car and was asleep by the time he made the ten-minute trip to the hospital. Inside, they looked over Rina's wound and decided that she needed rest and not blood.

Luke checked her into the hospital and followed her into the room. Bradley stationed a guard outside her door, and Luke stayed with her in the room. He called Sarah to let her know that she was okay, and to make sure that Sarah was staying somewhere safe.

In the meantime, Bradley had called the neighboring parishes to borrow their K9 units to track Del down. In addition, he borrowed Stewart from Mrs. Robichaux because Luke had said it was Stewart's barking that had woken him up and Stewart already knew Del's scent from when he chased him into the woods.

D el had already stolen a car, though, and was too far away to be scented by the dogs. He deposited his *accoutrements*, as he liked to call them, on the bed of the pay-by-the-hour motel in Lafayette. Stay calm, he told himself. He needed to think. Shit, shit, he had shot her. He would get nothing if he killed Rina. He had to figure out a way to get her alone and unharmed.

Luke was stuck like glue to her and apparently she wasn't teaching either. So how could he get her away from Luke? Luke, out of the picture, permanently, what a nice sound that was. Luke had been bedeviling him since he was 15. Butting in where he didn't belong. But if he could get rid of Luke, then Rina would be easy pickings. 'So the focus is changing,' he thought. 'Luke, you are now in my sights.'

$$23$$

"I'm losing my steam," Rina said out of the blue.

"What?"

"I'm just tired of this whole mess. I mean, c'mon. It is like everything is hanging in the balance, and we are just waiting for the next strike."

"Yeah, I know what you mean. It is annoying and aggravating. I think it is time to go from being hunted to hunting."

"I mean, basically, the idea has been that we entice Del to us, but if he is simply sneaking in, taking potshots, and then escaping; I don't see how our plan is succeeding."

"What we need," Rina said, "is a break, a way to find him. So, if you wanted to stay so you could continue to wreak havoc in the area, but you didn't want to be found in Meauxville, what would you do? Where would you go?"

"Lafayette. I could be anonymous in Lafayette. Not just there, but somewhere in the seedier parts of town, in the four corners area, maybe. Plus, there would be plenty of women there. Not to be indelicate, but Del liked to brag about his affinity for paying for his pleasure."

Rina gagged. "Ewwww! TMI."

"Well, it is helpful information. It could help us find him."

"So how would he get to Lafayette if he did not walk? Considering he thought gym class was beneath him, I would venture to guess that he didn't walk anywhere."

Luke considered for a moment. "Steal a car, a car from around here. Perhaps he stole a car and then drove there. Let's have Bradley check on stolen cars in the area. We'll get a list and then cruise the seedier motels to see if we can spot any of them."

"We will want a picture of Del as well," Rina added. "So that we can ask motels if they have seen him."

"I'll call Bradley. Maybe he'll want to take a road trip with us."

They picked up Bradley at the sheriff's station. "You got the stolen car makes, models and license plate numbers?" Luke asked.

"Yes, and I have a list of sleazy hotels. Plus, is it Festivals Acadiens, so there are very few hotels with vacancies, only the sleaziest hotels."

"Well, let's scope out three corners area and then get some food. I want a shrimp Po-boy from Old Tyme Grocery." Luke said.

"How can you think of food at a time like this?" Rina asked, appalled.

"Hey, we did not get breakfast, plus I barely ate yesterday worrying over your wound."

"I'm fine and to make you happy, I will rest on the way there." Rina leaned her head against Luke as he drove. She fell asleep instantly.

Luke looked in the rear-view mirror at Bradley. "So, should I take her to the safe house and then we can take off?"

"I would say yes, but 1) she would probably follow and 2) I don't trust Del to not follow us and then attack her, Bobby, and Sarah there." Luke grunted in agreement and kept driving.

Twenty minutes later, he took the exit off the I-10 and headed down Universal Drive. He went past the moderately priced hotels off the interstate and drove into town. Once he passed under the railroad tracks, he slowed the truck down. The Hour Pay Motel, Lafayette's busiest hourly rate motel, was right there after the railroad tracks. Luke turned into the motel's parking lot and began to cruise around looking for any of the cars on the list.

"Bingo," Bradley said, "Blue Dodge Caravan French plates. Silly Del, those are the easiest vanity plates to spot."

"Well, let's go in and see which room that *fils d'putain* is in," Luke said as he shook Rina awake.

When they showed the picture to the owner, they noticed the stray pain pills on his desk. They convinced him that providing them with Del's room number and a spare key was a smarter choice than jeopardizing his operation. By the end of their discussion, the manager was being as helpful as he could be.

Walking up to his room, they stopped when his door opened, and a woman staggered out. Her nose and her lip were bleeding and you could see the bruises forming on her wrists. She was halfway down the corridor when she stopped and saw them. "I hope you kill him," she whispered. "He has a gun on the night table and he has been doing something, I don't know what, but he's on something."

"Thanks," Rina whispered. The prostitute rolled her eyes until Luke handed her some bills.

"Thanks," he said. She smiled and moved in closer to him.

"Busy!" Rina stage-whispered and edged between Luke and the prostitute.

The woman rolled her eyes again and continued down the walkway.

As they went down the walkway, Luke and Bradley positioned themselves between Rina and the door. They got to the door, slipped in the key, and swung it open.

Del had apparently gone into the shower to wash off after his brutal session with the prostitute. The good news was that he did not take his gun into the shower with him. So Bradley and Luke gathered his gun and anything else he could use as a weapon and closed and locked his room door to ensure that he could not escape.

Del began singing Pat Benatar's 'Hurt so good' in the shower. "Could he be more hackneyed?" Rina whispered.

When the water turned off, all three of them went on alert. Del was whistling as he came out of the door with a towel wrapped around his waist.

"Hi Del!" Rina said cheerily. "How's it going?"

Del's eyes darted toward the nightstand where his gun had been.

"Oh, that's gone," Luke informed him. "Into the evidence bag to see if the bullets match the ones in my truck or the one that went through Rina's arm. I have a feeling it will. Plus, you will be happy to know that Porter is doing much better and singing like a canary. Boy, we can't get him to shut up. Apparently, he took offense to you trying to kill him."

"I don't know what you are talking about." Del eased towards Rina. Luke stepped between them and said, "I suggest that you don't move or else."

"Or else what bad boy? You think I'm scared of you?" Del sneered.

"Perhaps not," Bradley said from the opposite side of the room, "But you would do well to at least show respect for this." Del looked over and saw that Bradley had extracted his firearm and was currently pointing it at Del's head.

"Rina!" Del appealed to her. "You know I didn't do anything."

"You're kidding me, right? I was there when you ordered Porter to hurt me. I was there when you ran to the woods after you broke into my house. You are a *vaurien,* a good for nothing, and you have always been a *vaurien.* I regret the day that I ever met you."

Del looked like a cornered rat. He looked from Bradley to Luke to Rina, and then he darted towards Rina. Luke intercepted him just as he hit her newly bandaged gunshot wound. Rina screamed and automatically punched out with her other arm. She hit Del square in the eye and spun him around. It dazed him enough for Luke to start pounding on him.

As he hit, Luke enumerated all of Del's misdeeds. Luke added hits for other things in the past that Del had done to torment Rina. The list was long enough that Rina soon realized how long Luke had been looking out for her.

"Luke!" Rina shook herself out of her pain-induced daze and realized that Luke was nearly beating Del to death. Bradley was trying to pull Luke off Del, who looked like he was about to pass out.

Rina touched his arm. "Luke, please, I need you." Luke stopped, his breath heaving, his knuckles bruised, turning to see what she needed. She grabbed him and held on, waiting for the turmoil of the evening to subside.

24

B radley stepped in and cuffed Del. Del revived enough to cry, "Police brutality!"

"I'm not a cop," Luke informed Del. "Oh, and by the way, I married Rina, so your plan was shit from the start, *Couillon (Idiot)*."

"Plus, considering you tried to burn him out of his house. You tried to shoot him and you just punched Rina in the arm that you shot. It is going to be a cinch to prove self-defense. You, on the other hand, have no defense. If I were you, I would start planning for a long sojourn in jail. But the good news is you are going to be reunited with your old friend Porter. Yes, in fact, he specifically asked if you would be placed in the same prison as him. He is really looking forward to renewing your acquaintanceship," Bradley called for a patrol car.

"Okay ... let's go," Luke said to Rina. "I need to clean up, and you need to get some rest."

On the way out, they ran into their helpful street walker. She waited until Del passed and then spit in his face. "*Vaurien*," she said.

"See, that is what I call him," Rina agreed. "But I think *couillon* strikes harder considering that thinks he is completely brilliant."

She turned to Luke, saying, "I'm hungry. Let's go to Danny's so we can clean up, and then you can take me out to dinner."

"Sounds like a plan," Luke said. They watched Bradley shove Del into a squad car and then called to ask if he wanted to get something to eat. "No, I wanna get back to Sarah and Bobby to tell them the good news in person. Besides, I also want to walk this *vaurien* to the jail cell. The clang of the cell door will be sweet music to my ears."

Rina and Luke stopped by Danny's house to wash and prepare for dinner. "Where do you want to go eat?" Luke asked.

Rina bit her lower lip to think about it. She loved eating out. "I don't think I want sushi or Indian. I think nothing from the Asian continent tonight. No Thai, Chinese, Japanese, Indian, or Vietnamese. Oh I know, South American, Let's go to Guama's. You like their *plátanos* and I love their *Tuna a la Plancha*." Rina looked so excited about her choice, Luke couldn't refuse her anything.

After a relaxing dinner, both Luke and Rina were ready to retire. The drive home was soothing, and Rina fell asleep on Luke's shoulder. Luke carried her into the house, locked the door, and armed the alarm. He then carried her upstairs and tucked her into bed. Looking down on her as she slept, he wondered if she thought that she was now free. He smiled, curled around her, and went to sleep.

S arah woke up in Bradley's arms. He had gotten back late and then they stayed up late, discussing what had happened and what they would do now.

"I'm going to stay at *Chêne Vert*. Rina said that it is going to be half mine and I want to raise Bobby there."

"I'd like to stay there with you," Bradley said.

"We can't, you know that. Bobby can't see that his mom is shacking up."

"You know, if you would make an honest man of me, we wouldn't be shaking up."

"I can't."

"Why not Sarah?"

Sarah dropped her chin to her chest and shook her head. "I can't because I'm already married."

Bradley froze. "Excuse me?"

"I'm married. I left him. That was when I went away to college, but we never divorced."

Bradley jumped out of bed as if he had been burned. "Why?"

"Why didn't I tell you or why didn't I divorce?"

"Both."

"I didn't divorce because I don't know where he is, and I don't have the money to buy a divorce."

"I can find him and I can lend you the money. Boom! That problem is solved. Now for question number two. Why did you not tell me?"

Sarah hesitated, tears welling in her eyes. "I was ashamed."

"Why? Do you know how many people's first marriages fail? And you would have been married when you were, what ... 18? I can't think of anyone who married at 18 whose marriages lasted. It is not a big deal."

"No, not just that." Sarah got up and locked the door. "When I left, the last time I left Donald, he ... he claimed his husbandly rights against my wishes."

"He raped you. So, it wasn't after waking up from a party. A variation on your original story, but with an underlying truth. I'm going to kill him."

"You see, this is why I did not tell you. Plus, there is more. You remember when I arrived in town and then eight months later I had Bobby? That was when it happened. I just don't want to dwell on it. Bobby is the best thing that ever happened to me. How would I deal with him knowing how he was conceived? No, never gonna happen, so you can just forget about it, Bradley."

"Fine, we can keep that from surfacing. I still say we need to find Dickhead Donald and serve him divorce papers, or at the very least, you can divorce him *in absentia*."

"But I don't have any money. That will cost a fortune."

"Not a problem, you remember that I come from a long line of lawyers. I will get my father to do the honors in lieu of a marriage gift. Promise me you will come with me to speak with my father. I don't want to be without you. I don't want to run around and try to hide from Bobby that I'm sleeping with his mother. You know he is going to find out one day and then ask me what my intentions are. I will have to be honest with him."

Sarah closed her eyes, imagining what Bobby would do. "He will probably challenge you to a duel."

"No way, I will simply tell him I have offered to marry you numerous times, but that you are *tête dure (hard-headed)* and stubbornly refuse to capitulate. Then he and I will work systematically to bring you to the point."

"Oh God, you would, wouldn't you?" She buried her face in her hands.

"In a heartbeat, *ma belle (my beauty)*, in a heartbeat." Bradley kissed the side of her face and then got out his phone to call his father.

25

R ina woke with her head on Luke's shoulder. She opened her eyes, realized she was safe, and smiled. She then used her nose to play with his ears. Eventually, she nibbled on his earlobe and he began to stir.

Before he could come awake fully, Rina shifted her weight to fling her leg over Luke and then use the momentum so she could settle astride him. She peeled off her nightgown, that had shifted up over her hips, anyway. So, when Luke opened his eyes, he saw Rina's breasts full and swaying in front of his face.

"Good morning, Luke," Rina said.

Luke couldn't see her face, but the smile was in her tone. Luke simply licked her right nipple and then began to suckle and nibble, while his right hand began to fondle, weigh and then finally twirl her left nipple between his fingers. As he played with Rina's breasts, he ground his hips against her. The ridge in his boxer shorts worked against her ever-moist sheath. As he switched to nibble and suckle the left breast, his right hand worked its way down Rina's body to her waist, over her hip, and around her *derrière*. He found his way to her wetness. One finger entered her and then another. Luke anchored himself with his hand insider her as he switched from breast to breast.

Rina was crazy now, kicking, wriggling, and writhing. Luke took his hands off of her for a second as he ripped off his boxers. Then he settled Rina against him, entering her swiftly. One of his hands squeezed her ass while the other found her clit and began to twirl it between his thumb and forefinger.

As he worked her inside, behind, and in front, his mouth took hers, mimicking the movement below, with his tongue swirling in and out of her mouth. He began licking, nibbling and sucking her lips as Rina held his tongue in her mouth and began to suck. The suction was getting stronger as her pussy began to expand and contract tighter, ever tighter, on Luke's dick.

Rina didn't know if she was breathing. She felt Luke everywhere as her body writhed and throbbed, and wound like a spring until her body arched up, exploding. Her pussy contracted hard as she felt Luke shudder and flood inside her. She collapsed as his hands began a gentle caress up and down her sides.

"Mine," Rina mumbled, immediately falling back to sleep. Luke smiled and thought, 'Back at ya.'

Rina woke up hours later beside cool sheets. She could hear Luke banging around in the kitchen, but she just couldn't find the energy to roll out of bed. She brushed her hair back from her face as she angled the pillows to allow her to recline in bed and finish her book. As she read, her eyes kept straying to her ring finger with her non-existent wedding ring.

She really did not have any right to hold Luke to his promise. He had married her to try to keep her safe, but still, it was not like he had to do that. Besides, he didn't have to make love to her and he sure as heck had been doing that since they got married. What did he think, that he could just marry her and then take advantage of her? Rina's thoughts began to spiral, and she frantically tried to come up with reasons that Luke would have to stay with her.

Luke came into the room smiling and carrying a tray of breakfast. He stopped short at the door when he saw the fury on Rina's face.

"What?! You think you can just marry me, have sex with me, and then leave me? Just because I'm safe doesn't mean that you can renege on your word. You signed on that line, just like me. You're stuck, buddy!" Rina's lower lip came out in an enticing pout.

"Okay, I'm good with that," Luke said and set the tray in front of her.

"Okay, you can't just say 'okay'. You have to be angry that I'm trying to keep you married against your wishes. You have to resign yourself to the millions and try to find comfort there. You can't just say 'okay'."

"Actually, I've already put my half of the money in a college fund for *les petits.*"

"What *petits*? Do you have children, and you never told me? I think that is something I should have been told," Rina continued, knowing she sounded crazy but unable to keep the insanity from her lips.

Luke smiled, "I might."

"You might ... you don't know? Are you saying you are going around having unprotected sex and then coming home and making love to me?"

"God no! I have only had unprotected sex with you. Two times now, so the answer to 'if I have children' is a, maybe. When will we find out?"

Rina's hand slipped to her belly. "Oh." She hadn't really thought of that. "I ...I ... I ... in a two or three weeks."

"Excellent, I will let you know in two or three weeks if I have any children that will be using their newly established college fund," Luke said, and he turned to walk back to the kitchen.

"But Luke, you don't want to marry me," Rina said, grabbing her robe and her coffee and following him.

"I already have married you."

"I mean, you didn't want to marry me."

"If you will recall, I was the one that called Mr. Trahan and asked him to look over the will. And when he told me what he found, I was the one that arranged our marriage. It was actually all a ruse to ensure that you married me."

"You are insane!"

"No doubt. Want some more toast? Your coffee is getting cool." He poured some more coffee into her cup. Rina bit into her toast and looked at Luke as if he were up to something, while Luke projected innocence as well as he could.

They were locked in a stare for a few minutes until Bobby broke their stalemate by flinging open the kitchen door. "We're back!" he said, striking a pose. Then he ran to his uncle and new aunt and hugged them. "Did you miss me, Tante Rina?" he asked.

"Enormously!" Rina smiled.

"Did you go somewhere?" Luke teased. "I thought you were just hiding out in your tree house."

"My tree house! I need to make sure that *fils d'putain* Del did not mess anything up." And he rushed out to the backyard as his mom, who had come in after him, yelled, "Language!"

Bradley laughed, "That wasn't me! That was Nonc Luke!"

"I'll let it slide only because Del is certainly a *fils d'putain*. Although, I really never had anything against his mother. She just always seemed so shy and restrained."

"No doubt beaten into submission by Del's daddy," Bradley stated.

The screen door opened to a worried Bobby. "Ah, will you come with me, Nonc Luke? I'm not scared or anything, but he might have left behind clues or something."

"Yeah, kid. You never know, and besides, I haven't been up there in ages." Luke headed out to see about the tree house as Bradley, Sarah, and Rina smiled after them. Rina started the dishes as Bradley picked up his hat to head out.

✦

26

"Well, I'm off to see about a divorce," Bradley said, and then turned to leave.

"A divorce? Bradley is married?" Rina asked.

Bradley, realizing what he had let slip, stopped in his tracks.

"No." Sarah's eyes darted away.

"Spill!" Rina prodded. "Who is getting divorced?"

Sarah took a deep breath and then exhaled slowly.

"I am."

Rina stopped washing the dishes and slowly turned around. "Excuse me? Did you just say that you are married?"

"And on that note, I'm heading out," Bradley said, escaping out the kitchen door.

"Rina, you can't tell Luke. He would be so upset," Sarah pleaded. "I was so ashamed. Donald was not kind. I got away, but I was alone and apparently at the time pregnant—which I soon found out. I had nowhere to go, so I just went back home."

"Well, of course you came home. Where else would you go? We would have been heartbroken if we thought that you did not think you could rely on us. So … uh … where's this Donald bastard?"

"Don't know, don't care," Sarah said. "I left him. Then I went home and I haven't had the time or the money to divorce him. Bradley was a little upset when he found out he had been cavorting with a married woman. Needless to say, he is eager for me to divorce Donald."

"You're not telling me everything," Rina said. "What aren't you telling me?"

"It's not important," Sarah said and went to get some coffee.

"If it is unimportant, then you would not be working so hard to hide it. Give, Sarah."

"Like I said, Donald was not … kind to me. He hurt me, but he is gone and he is not coming back, so there is no need to …"

"I'm going to kill him. Bradley is going to find him and then I'm going to kill him. He and I are going to take a walk down the Poisoner's Corridor."

Sarah smiled, "You are a blood-thirsty wench. No wonder Luke loves you. Fine, we will plan on Donald dying a horribly gruesome and painful death. But for today, let's do something that does not involve violence. I'm kinda tired of that. Let's do something fun. Bowling and beer?" Sarah suggested.

"**N**o!" Luke said emphatically as he walked back in, clearly just hearing the last bit of the conversation.

Sarah gave Rina a shut-up look and turned to Luke. "Fine, sore loser," Sarah retorted.

"How about some *Bourré*?" Rina asked, as Luke went to get some coffee.

"Penny ante?" Sarah asked.

"Chump change," Luke said. "Nickel ante and quarter *Bourré*."

"Yes! Call Bradley and let him know. *Bourré* tonight!" Rina ran to get her cards and her change.

Bobby came back in as they were setting up the card table. "Are we playing cards?"

"*Bourré*, tonight," Sarah told him.

"Woo hoo! I rock at *Bourré*. Let me get my change." And he, too, ran up the stairs.

Sarah turned to look at Luke. "How does my son know how to gamble?"

"I don't know if I would count penny ante *Bourré* as gambling. Besides, it is an important aspect of his cultural heritage. Like the French, you won't let me teach him."

"That you teach him, anyway," Sarah teased.

"Only because it is self-defense. He needs to know if someone is insulting him in French."

"*Bourré* works up an appetite," Rina interjected. "Y'all gonna want some?" She phoned her cousin, Danny, to pick up some Marie LaVeau pizzas at DeanO's pizza and join them for *Bourré* that night.

That evening, Rina and Sarah made some Zatarain's root beer while they waited for Danny to bring the pizza. They played *Bataille*, a. k. a. War, with Bobby while they waited with Luke and Bradley, taking turns after they turned over each card in the deck. Bobby rushed to the window when he heard Danny driving up. "Pizza, pizza!" he squealed as he opened the door for Danny.

Danny came in, deposited the pizza on the kitchen table and then went to give Rina a big hug. "Hey cuz. I hear you've been beating up bad guys, marrying a badass, and making use of my digs while I was away. Mom says she will be planning a huge reception party when she gets back from Florida. She said if all it took was getting someone to attack Rina to get you two together, she would have hired a thug ages ago."

Rina rolled her eyes and went to get some plates for the pizza. Danny held out his hand to Luke. "Welcome to the family."

"Thanks," Luke shook his hand.

"And you," Danny yelled over at Bobby, who had frozen in the act of eating the pizza without the requisite plate or napkin, "you can call me Cousin Danny now. Your family has grown exponentially, hasn't it?"

"Yes," Bobby said, "and I can't wait until I get some new cousins." He looked over at Rina.

"We're working on it, kid," Luke said.

"Luke!" Rina scolded. "One does not discuss such things at the dinner table."

"But Rina, this is the *Bourré* table. One discusses whatever one likes at the *Bourré* table," Bradley said. "So about those kids. Y'all didn't waste any time. Did you? And here Sarah thought you were married in name only."

"Bradley!" Sarah exclaimed. "Is there any way to shut you up?"

"*Un tit bec doux,* that will do."

"What's a ..." Sarah tried to ask before Bradley kissed her gently to show her. "Ohh ..."

"Mr. Bradley, when Mom finally decides to make an honest man of you, can I call you 'Dad'?" Bobby asked after Bradley finished his kiss. "Bradley!"

"Sure thing, kid, and then I can teach you all my French moves so you can use them on the girls."

"Ewwww ... why would I want to do that? Girls are gross!"

"They get better with age," Luke said.

"If you say so," Danny chimed in.

"Your opinion doesn't count."

"What! I am hurt and shocked that you are denying me a voice. I like girls, they go shopping, and go see sappy movies, and they always dance," Danny said.

"Seriously?! Those have to be their worst qualities!" Bradley said.

"You appreciate girls your way and I'll appreciate them mine," Danny retorted.

"Just as long as you all appreciate us!" Rina said. "Now ante up and cut the cards. It is time to play."

27

L uke cut, Rina dealt, and then turned over her fifth card to reveal an ace of hearts as the trump.

"Nice draw, bitch!" Sarah said.

"Mom, language," Bobby teased.

"Now, now … the rest of my cards might be *merde*. How many you trading in?"

"Give us five." Sarah and Bobby were playing with the same hand.

"Sarah, we have been over this. You can fold and not play if your hand is that bad."

"Sit there doing nothing to save myself a quarter? I don't think so. Gimme five cards."

"Fine." Rina dealt to Sarah, and the others traded in their unwanted cards. When they were done, Rina looked at her cards. She had ace, king, queen of hearts, and then two useless cards. She threw out the two weak cards and dealt herself two more. Ace of spades and four of hearts. Rina flipped her hair over her shoulders to prepare to play.

"I'm out!" Luke said. "Every time you do that hair flipping thing, you kick our butts."

"You can't fold now. You can only do that when you have your original hand. You traded in cards, so you are playing. Now prepare to *Bourré*." Sarah and Bobby led with a diamond and Rina won the trick with her four of hearts.

Then Rina played her ace of spades, "Ride baby ride," she asked the cards and apparently everyone had spades, so that was trick number two.

Then she smiled and laid down her ace, king, queen, and everyone just groaned and threw their hands at her.

"How do you do it? You are like the *Bourré* queen."

"It's a gift," Rina said. "Now everyone put in your quarters, and I'll see if I can win a bigger pot. Mama wants a new pair of shoes."

Bradley whispered in Bobby's ear. "*Beque mon tchu!* Tante Rina," Bobby said, and then turned to a smiling Bradley, and asked, "Did I say it right?"

Rina smiled and said, "Indeed you did, Bobby, but don't use that language at school."

"Bradley Everett Trahan, what are you teaching my son?" Sarah scolded.

"Well now, Sarah, I'm disappointed in you. I just taught you what *tits becs doux* is? Do you need me to remind you again?"

Sarah's face flushed. "No, I remember, but why can't Bobby say 'kiss' at school?"

"It is not the kissing that is going to get Bobby in trouble, it is what he told Rina to kiss," Danny smirked as he tattled.

"Bradley!" Sarah said.

"*Beque mon tchu! Beque mon tchu!*" Bobby repeated, to make sure he did not lose that valuable phrase.

"Ante up!" Rina said. "Bradley, it is your deal."

"Geez, is she always like this?" Bradley asked Danny.

"Rina and I come from a long line of *Bourré* champions," Danny stated. "Sit back and watch our card splendor."

Rina rolled her eyes. "Hit me with one."

"Crap, how do you only need one? I need five," Luke said.

"Language, and if you haven't noticed, there appears to be a direct positive correlation between taking five cards and *Bourréing*."

"Is *Bourréing* a word? And, no, I haven't noticed," Luke said.

"You will. Sarah, it is your and Bobby's turn to play."

"Yes ma'am," Sarah saluted and laid down her king of spades.

"I have a very important question to ask. Actually, I have two very important questions to ask," Danny said when it got to his turn.

"Sarah played a spade and hearts are trump." Rina responded automatically.

"*Merci bien*." And then Danny played his heart and won the trick.

"Wow," Bobby said. "It is like Tante Rina can read minds."

"More like Tante Rina has played *Bourré* with me enough to know that I have the short-term memory of a gnat," Danny told him.

Bobby snickered. "I love playing *Bourré* over here. It is much more fun than our house."

"Hey!" Luke said, "I can't believe you are dissing our *Bourré* game." He feigned a hurt expression.

"Well, we don't play with pizza and homemade root beer, and you never taught me French cursing when we played it at home," Bobby argued.

"I'm trying not to feel insulted." Luke grumbled, "but it's hard."

"Ah Nonc Luke," Bobby said, "Playing a game with just your uncle, that is what losers do."

"Are you trying to make me feel better or worse?" Luke asked, refusing to put him out of his misery.

"Besides," Rina interjected, "this is your home now, so you are playing at home with pizza and root beer, so home is definitely not the boring element in the equation. Which means there was only one other variable that could have made it boring. It's the scientific method of deduction." And she gave an exaggerated stare in Luke's direction.

"I am not boring." Luke said. "I can make you take that back." Rina blushed.

"Oh pray tell, how will you make Rina take it back?" Sarah asked, newly interested in the conversation.

"Never mind." Luke said.

Bradley chimed in. "Now, now, you can't just throw that out there and then take it back. That is very unkind. Now describe, in detail, how you are going to make Rina renounce her statement that you are a dullard."

"I didn't call him a dullard. Besides, need I remind everyone that we have an impressionable child in the room?"

"See mom, this is so much more fun."

"Bobby darlin', do you know how to make the root beer by yourself?" Danny asked.

"Yes, and I know exactly the amount of syrup to put in the water to make a full gallon of root beer."

"What a talent! Well, why don't you go off to the kitchen and make us some more root beer? We'll take our 7th inning *Bourré* stretch, and then we can find out how your Nonc Luke thinks to get your Tante Rina, to take back her insult." Danny smirked.

"Okay!" Bobby said and got up to leave.

"Oh, no you don't. You are staying right here and enjoying the company of everyone else. Then, instead of root beer, Tante Rina will fix you her special hot chocolate with the cayenne and the marshmallows. Sound good, Bobby?"

"Yes," and he turned to his mom, "best day ever!"

Sarah smiled and said, "Well, your uncle and aunt set the bar high."

28

They played another few rounds while the stack of coins in front of Rina grew and everyone else's, except for Danny's, shrunk. Danny held his own, but he was no match for Rina.

"I don't know why we needed a huge dowry. I could have gotten just as rich with you as a card shark," Luke told Rina.

"Dowry? What dowry?" Danny asked.

"Well, that is sort of what started all the trouble with Del. Apparently, Pawpaw left me with a dowry and only a man from one of the founding families of Meauxville could claim it. It was the reason Luke had to marry me—to try to get Del to stop trying to kidnap and marry me," Rina said.

"No, the reason I married you was because I finally found my in. All I had to do was get some lunatic to attack you and you would finally fall into my arms."

"Seriously, that was why Del went after you? I used to think that boy was sharp, but he is a few cards short of a full deck," Danny said.

Bobby snickered and repeated the insult, "a few cards short of a full deck" to himself.

"Why do I have the feeling a call from the school informing me that Bobby got in trouble is imminent?" Sarah asked. "God knows what he will say when he gets to school on Monday."

"It is only imminent because he's related to Luke," Rina said. "So, when do you start school for your teaching certificate?" As she spoke, she scooped up another trick.

"How do you do that? I'll start next semester. I found an alternative program that will offer me an online bachelor's degree in criminal justice, then it will allow me to get a master's degree and certification. Grad school and a degree. I'm so excited!"

Rina hugged Sarah. "That's great," she said as she picked up another trick. "That's just amazing."

"Okay, last round. I need to keep money for the laundromat," Danny explained.

After Rina won the last round, the party split up. Sarah went to put Bobby to bed. Bradley went to go and make up the couch, and Danny kissed Rina while he stole some change from her.

"You thief!" Rina ran after him.

"Darling, you have more than enough with your 'dowry' and all. Plus, tomorrow is laundry day and I am a fashion whore. I can't wear the same outfit twice, so it makes for piles and piles of laundry." Danny blew her some kisses as he climbed into his car.

Rina and Luke stopped to speak with Bradley on the way up. "You know that Sarah is staying in what was once the master suite," Rina told him.

"It is pretty snazzy," Bradley agreed.

"What you may not know about the master suite is that it was built in the early 19th century."

"Interesting history lesson Rina, but you know, I was a criminal justice major."

"Men are so difficult. Bradley, did you know that in the 1700s and 1800s upper-class men and women did not share a room? They had a master's suite and a mistress' suite so that both of them had their separate quarters, but there was a door connecting both the suites. We turned our mistress' suite into a guest bedroom and I'm wondering if, instead of sleeping on the couch, you would like to sleep in the guest room. The one with the connecting door to Sarah's room. Is that enough explanation for you? Men!" Rina harrumphed.

Bradley smiled. "So I get to be the mistress?"

"You are a kept man. Until she makes an honest man of you, that is," Rina responded.

Bradley undid the bedding on the couch and gathered it up. "Lead on," he gestured. He had a bigger smile on his face when Sarah came out to see what the noise was.

"We are just letting Bradley use the guest bedroom. He can't sleep on the couch. Tante D would be affronted with such a lack of hospitality," Rina told her.

Sarah's eyes sparkled. "Well, we couldn't have that."

Rina hugged Luke's arm as they continued on to their room. "Feel like a good Samaritan, do you?" Luke asked.

"Yes, a good Samaritan with many, many coins."

"Arcade tomorrow after school?" Luke asked.

"Why do I feel transported back to the 80s? Are we going to the roller rink? Will I get to wear spandex and a headband? I know I can still kick your ass in Asteroids."

"Okay, that was a onetime fluke," Luke argued as they went into their room.

The next day, Bradley was in the interrogation room when they brought in Del.

"So dumbass, you were trying to get a married lady to marry you so that you could get her dowry. What are you, an 18th century arch villain? Could you be any dumber?"

'Bingo!' Bradley thought. He saw the rage immediately. If there was one thing that Del despised, it was being called unintelligent.

"I'm afraid I will have to ask you to call my lawyer. I really have nothing to say to you," Del countered, keeping his anger in check. Bradley nodded to Richard to call the lawyer.

"In the meantime, dipshit, I have a phone call to make," said Bradley. "So, you just stay quiet while I talk to Luke. Hey Luke, yeah we've got him. He lawyered up, so I'm just calling you while we wait for his lawyer to arrive. Can you believe his idiocy? I mean seriously, does he think that Porter was not going to tell us anything? Or had he hoped that little blow to the head would kill him? Tried to kill his best friend. What *basse classe* ... always knew he was trash. He's not just stupid, but a wimp too. I wonder how he ever got to be a bully. I mean, I understand the dumb part. A lot of bullies are making up for their inadequacies in the smarts department, but he doesn't have brains or brawn. What was he thinking? Or maybe he just wasn't thinking."

Del said nothing, but his face was turning beet red. He started to sputter. Bradley turned at the noise to address him.

"No, no, don't talk. Remember, you lawyered up." He turned his back to Del again and resumed his conversation with Luke. "I'm sure he wasn't thinking. Too bad for him. Wait until he hears what his once best friend told us before we allowed him to walk out the door."

Del overturned the chair as he stood up. "What did he tell you?" he demanded to know.

Bradley addressed him, "Now Del, we are waiting for your lawyer. We can't talk to you unless you waive your rights to a lawyer. Now sit back down and we will wait."

He went back to his conversation with Luke. "Yep, what Porter gave us was so good that we don't even need a statement. He is, in fact, on his way to go and apologize to Rina and let

Luke take a crack at him because he knows that what he has done is wrong, and he has repented."

Del stood again, and Bradley calmed him. "Now, don't get that look in your eye, Del. So what if Porter is getting off scot free while you will be spending some quality time in lockdown?"

The momentary gleam in Del's eyes dimmed. "Fine, I'll talk to you."

Bradley hung up the phone on Luke's answering machine. "Great, let's talk about the silver. You see, we knew that you wanted Rina's dowry. Then your friend Porter shed a whole new light on the entire episode. He said that you were looking for a list of items. Now, what I need is that list."

Del looked at him and smiled his treacherous smile.

"Oh no, don't get that happy look. This is not a get-out-of-jail-free card. This is a don't-be-put-in-the-cell-with-Killer-McCleod moment. This way, Del, you might actually survive your multiple prison terms."

"I have the list," Del responded. "What can I get for it?"

"Now Del, you know you asked for your lawyer don't you want to wait for them before you make a deal?"

"Screw my lawyer. I don't want my lawyer. I want to talk to you. So what can you offer me?"

"You can get an all-expense-paid trip to Angola, but instead of being in the murderer's row, we can put you in with tamer criminals. Judging by the age of the prostitute the other night, you would probably do well with the pedophiles."

"I want promises. I need it in writing."

"We wouldn't have it any other way, Del. Of course, that will entail a confession, as well. Not that we need one, considering half the sheriff's force saw you try to gun down Rina and Luke, and Rina was there when you invaded her home."

"I don't know what you are talking about."

"Plus, you were such an arrogant dumbass you didn't even notice that she had dialed 911. We have the entire conversation on tape, and a 911 operator who can corroborate Rina's testimony. So, confession first, and then the list of articles that you think contain the antebellum silver."

"Fine, give me some paper."

Bradley handed Del a pad and pen. Del wrote out his confession on one page, and on another listed the articles he believed contained the LeBlanc family silver.

"Alrighty. We will turn you over to the prison system, and you enjoy the rest of your life behind bars."

"This isn't over yet, Bradley."

"Oh, I'm afraid it is. You will not be leaving Angola except in a pine box."

29

B radley, Luke, Rina, and Sarah met over hot chocolate, and some pound cake Rina had made. Bobby was already in bed with the promise that he would get a slice of the cake for breakfast with hot chocolate.

Luke took a bite of the cake and a sip of the chocolate. "A moment of silent reverence so the pleasure of eating and drinking this feast can sink in." They all took a bite of cake and a sip of the chocolate and closed their eyes.

Sarah giggled. "It really is delicious, Rina."

"*C'est bon*," Bradley corrected.

"Thanks, but let's get to the business at hand. Bradley, you have the list?"

Bradley pulled out the list of articles that were bequeathed to Rina in the will. "And Del thinks that somewhere in this list is Tante D's antebellum silver? Okay...who else besides me thinks this is stupid?" Rina asked. All three of the others raised their hands.

"But, for Tante D's sake, I still say we should check out those items," Sarah said.

"Fine, just tell me what you need me to do, and I will do it," Luke said as he scarfed down the pound cake and washed it down with hot chocolate.

Rina took little sips as she thought about the logistics of the task. Luke watched her savor her hot chocolate, think and then close her eyes as she ate a bite of pound cake.

"*Gourmande*, (someone who loves food)" Luke thought. He loved that about Rina. She wasn't a diet lifestyle type of girl. She had given up dieting a long time ago and now she was just Rina. She ate what she wanted, when she wanted. She savored when she wanted to savor and devoured when she wanted to devour.

As his food fantasies began to morph into bedroom fantasies, Rina's voice interrupted. "Luke, are you listening to me?" she asked with her hands on her hips and a pout on her lips.

"Of course," Luke said.

"Then what did I just say?" Rina asked.

"Teachers ..." Luke grumbled, "I don't remember."

"I really should write you up, but I will punish you later."

"Really?!" Luke perked up. "I can't wait. So, what did you say?"

"I said that Bradley and Sarah can go to the *garconnière* (attic) and see if they can find the chest, the jewelry box, and the fur coats. I think that is the most logical place to find those items. Look for a cedar closet or chest for the furs. In the meantime, you and I will go and look for the artillery chest, the foyer bench, and the armoire. The ones that Momma left me are probably in some of the guest rooms."

They split up and went to search the house. Sarah and Bradley went up to the attic. Sarah carried flashlights and a fly swatter. "You see, this is what happens when we allow Rina to assign tasks. She knows I hate spiders, but she hates them too, so look who gets stuck braving the spiders in the attic!" Sarah complained.

"But you have big, brave Bradley to protect you," Bradley said from behind her. He couldn't see it, but he could feel her rolling her eyes.

The attic was a mess of old boxes, covered furniture, and dust. Sarah and Bradley carefully uncovered the furniture, trying not to emit too much dust into the atmosphere.

L uke and Rina started with the unoccupied guest rooms. They found several chests, benches, and armoires, but none had a stash of silver and none were the objects described in will that were bequeathed to Rina.

They went to the occupied rooms next. Luke's room was nearly empty. He had moved all of his things into Rina's room since the wedding. Except for some odd books and random tools, he only had an armoire and nothing else.

Rina looked under his bed. "Hey wait, there seems to be a box of some sort under here. Did you store something underneath your bed?"

"Nope, everything I had was in my suitcase."

"Yeah! Maybe we found something," Rina wiggled under the bed up to her rear. Luke just admired the view as she was squirming around, trying to pull out the box.

"This thing is heavy," she said and squirmed back and forth, trying to pull or push the box out. Luke was really starting to enjoy himself when Rina squirmed back out.

"I'm sorry Luke, I was speaking clearly, but sometimes I forget to speak 'Man'. Let me rephrase. The box is heavy. You are stronger than me and you are here to help me with my task. Therefore, I need you to get under the bed and help me get the box."

"Oh! Well, why didn't you just say so?" Luke asked.

Rina shook her head and smiled. Then she just stared at Luke's firm little ass until he came out with the box about a minute later.

"Oh boy, oh boy, oh boy!" Rina jumped up and actually clapped her hands.

Luke shook his head. "You really are excited about this, aren't you?" he asked.

"Yes, I mean, I know it is a crock. I know we aren't going to find anything, but I love the quest. I love searching for things and seeing if I can solve problems and mysteries and riddles. That's why I love..."

"The Magic of Chemistry," Luke finished for her (including the flourished hand gestures).

"Damn straight! Now pop this box open because I say it is an artillery case, probably from the First World War. It looks old."

They opened the case to find some old pistols, older than World War I. In fact, the pistols looked like dueling pistols from the early 19th century.

"Jackpot," Rina said. "This stuff is old enough. What else have we got in here?"

Luke pulled out an old leather-bound journal with yellowing pages. "French," he said as he flipped through it.

"Let me see that," Rina said and flipped through the pages. "*La guerre de septs ans!!!* That's it! That is the war of succession, as Tante D calls it," Rina continued reading. "It is hard to read. The way they write letters is different, but I think, based on the handwriting, that this is a journal of a female member of the family. There is a lot in here about the neighboring families and dresses and handsome soldiers. Okay ... now we just have to find where it is talking about Union soldiers. It was right before the Union soldiers used *Chêne Vert* as their base that the silver would have been hidden. Here it is. They had just fought outside of Sunset. So, the writer and her cousin began to hide things. Oh my God, there is a list of where they hid things. I don't know how much it will help, though. The third magnolia past the slave quarters. That's where they hid the platters. Not sure where that is. The cutlery was hidden in the secret compartment in the armoire, so we still need to find that. They hid the jewels in their clothes, so that means that the fur coats might have some jewels in them. It doesn't say anything about a bench, though. Where do you think Del got his information? It seems to have some sort of basis in fact."

"Who was the cousin?" asked Luke. "The one that hid the items with your great, great, great grandma? There were not that many families here at the time and yours and Del's were founding families. I'm guessing that somewhere along the line, her family married into Del's and they have perhaps one of her cousin's journals."

"Oh, this is sooo cool. We might actually have some real clues to the treasure. Tante D always did say it was somewhere."

30

S arah and Bradley came back covered in dust and cobwebs. "We might have found something," Bradley said, as Sarah rushed to the sink to try to wash off her face and hands and also some of her hair.

"We found better!!" Rina said.

"Always so competitive," Luke smiled. "Our discovery is certainly impressive, but you go first."

"We found an armoire. It seems to match the description in the will," Sarah said, pleased with herself.

"Yeah, the cutlery is probably in there. In the secret compartment!" Rina exclaimed.

"The cutlery?" asked Sarah.

"Secret compartment?" Bradley and Sarah looked confused.

"That is our find," Luke said. "We found a journal that details where Rina's great, great, great grandmother and aunt hid all the valuables. The cutlery was hidden in the armoire in a secret compartment."

"So let's go up to the *garconnière* and see if we can find it," Rina said, running up the stairs.

"Fun," Sarah exclaimed half-heartedly. She looked a bit put out that she had to return to the spidery attic.

Once in the attic, Bradley directed them to the armoire. One by one Rina and Sarah took out all the drawers. Bradley and Luke kept tapping on the armoire to see if they could hear a hollow compartment. They then studied all the drawers. Nothing. Not a fork.

Rina, in frustration, started shaking the drawers. After the third drawer, Sarah stopped her. "Wait," Sarah told her, "Shake that one again."

Rina did, and there was a slight tapping sound heard. Rina examined the box again. Then she examined the other boxes. It looked like this box was made out of thicker wood. However, when she tapped on the wood of the rattling box, it gave a hollow thump. "This is it!" she yelled, and she started to carefully, pry off the end of the drawer.

"You do know that's an antique and that Tante D will literally kill you if you destroy it," Luke reminded her.

"Not if I find the treasure," Rina said. "Besides, I know that Tante D's wrath is a bunch of malarkey. She's as soft as they come. You will remember that I am the person that blew up my bedroom, in addition to the basement, and yet I am still standing and breathing."

"Yes, but she did not have antiques in your room or the basement. Tante D knew better than to put you in close proximity to valuable objects," Sarah countered.

Rina stuck out her tongue at Sarah and continued to pry off the end of the drawer. She was finally able to dislodge the end when about two collections of cutlery fell clanging to the floor.

"Hot damn! She was right!" Bradley said.

Rina wasn't completely happy. "Let's check the other drawers. I mean, this was the 18th century. There should be about 20 sets of cutlery at the minimum."

"Perhaps they did not want the Union to think that they had hid all the silver, so they left the rest out and just kept back some," Sarah reasoned.

"That seems logical. Still, they would have not thought that cutlery for two would be enough to save. There has to be more."

They found two more drawers with false compartments and finished with six sets of cutlery.

"Yay! With all of us and Tante D, we have enough for all of us for Thanksgiving. Tante Ds is going to be soooo happy to be eating off of the heirloom silverware! I have to call her!" Rina ran from the room, with Sarah following.

Bradley and Luke bent to pick up all the silver. "I guess she is excited about finding the family silver. Unfortunately, we will be the ones polishing it," Bradley said.

"No doubt," Luke said, but he was smiling, anyway. He heard Rina on the phone. "Yes, Tante D, I know it is late. No, nothing is wrong. Yes, you taught me better than this. I know … I am impossible to teach manners, but Sarah is calling too. No, I'm not putting her on the phone. I get to talk to you first. Yes, I know it has been a while. But, but … Tante D, listen. Yes, but …"

Sarah took the phone out of Rina's hands and yelled, "Tante D, we found the silver!!"

Rina tried not to grimace because she did not get to tell her aunt, but she could hear the excitement four feet from the phone.

Sarah continued, "Here's Rina. She is the one who figured out where it was."

Rina kissed Sarah on the cheek and then took the phone. "Oh, so now you want me to talk? Before I couldn't get a word in what with all the scolding. No, you can't take me over your knee. No, you can't get Luke to do it either."

"Yes, she can!!" Luke yelled down the stairs. Rina narrowed her eyes at him with no heat.

"So, here is how we found it and what we have left to find. Of course, we could wait a day if you wanted to come and … Oh, so you are coming back tomorrow. How unexpected." Rina winked at Sarah.

Over the next week, they all got together to try to find the rest of the treasure. To find the platters, they had to find out where the slave quarters had been and the configurations of the trees. It was Bobby who suggested that they find some old photographs of the house. "Why don't you look at those old photos that Tante D is always making me look at? There were bunches of trees in there and those old run-down shacks."

Sarah questioned Tante D. She had some old photos, but most of them were at the library. Plus, all the old property specs and descriptions of the land and edifices were at city hall.

Bradley looked at city hall after work and found the exact coordinates of the slave/sharecropper quarters about 25 years after the platters were hidden. Sarah and Bobby went to the library to find old pictures of the house, while Tante D went through her photo albums and found all her old photos of the house.

Rina, with her scientific mind, created a proportionately accurate diorama from all the old pictures. She also looked up magnolia trees to find out how far apart they often grew and also, in case they had been planted, how far apart they were traditionally planted at the end of the 18th century at other plantations. Based on all of that information, they created a grid at the northeast end of the house where the slave quarters had been and created a grid that matched the diorama.

They created hypotheses to try to figure out where the platters could be, and then, as they were coming up with a plan to dig, Bobby again interjected. "Why don't you just use my metal detector to see if they are down there? Won't it detect silver?" A pin could have dropped in the room.

"Yes, Sarah, why don't we just use the metal detector?" Bradley asked snidely.

"Oh hush! Bobby, that is a great idea."

"Okay, Bobby, this is your big moment. Here is the grid. We think it could be in one of these four squares. Can you go out with your metal detector and start in this area to see if you can hear anything?"

"I could," Bobby said, "But I'm really hungry and thirsty."

"Well, are you going to starve the poor boy?" Tante D asked. "Here Sweetie, Tante D made you some cookies. You go out there with this cookie, and I will make you some hot cider."

"Thanks Tante D," Bobby smiled beatifically at her.

"Cher bébé, you are so sweet."

Bobby raced outside.

"Little extortionist." Rina muttered, "I wonder where he gets it from." She looked directly at Luke.

"It is not extortion to ask a customer to pay for services rendered." Luke said.

"I have been paying," Rina said. "$50 a week."

"Okay, you know you have nearly four million dollars in the bank, right?"

"I'm saving it for Bobby and our little whose-it."

There was complete silence.

"I'm sorry. Did you just tell me you are pregnant?"

"Must I speak man-speak all the time? Yes, I can't spend money on a car that you should just give to me because I need to make sure Bobby and our child, which is even now as we speak growing in my stomach, have enough money for the crazy school bills. Plus, I'm paying for Sarah's education, too."

"You are not! I am paying my own way!" Sarah exclaimed.

"No, you are going to be a full-time student. You aren't going to work."

"Yes, I am," Sarah said. "I'm working part time."

"I'm paying for her education," Luke argued. "And you are going to school full-time!"

"No, you are not." Sarah argued.

"Well, then you are taking a cut of the profits when we sell the silver," Rina said.

"What!!" Tante D yelled. "Over my dead body will you sell our heirloom silver!"

"Of course they aren't selling the silver, Tante D. I will make sure that it stays in the family, no matter what," Sarah said, narrowing her eyes at Rina for upsetting Tante D.

"Of course you will, dear, and because you won't be getting any money for all your and Bobby's work to help us find it, you will, of course, allow me to pay for your schooling."

Sarah sputtered, "Now, now," Tante D said, "No need to thank me. I'm happy to do it. It gives me something to look forward to and be happy about in these, my final years on the planet. Just knowing that I will be giving something back by investing in your education is thanks enough. Well, I think I've had enough excitement for tonight. Rina, be a dear, and take this cider out to Bobby."

And with that, Tante D started up the stairs to bed. "Wake me when you find the platters," she called down to them. Sarah stood stunned for a few minutes.

When Rina got back from delivering the cider to Bobby, Sarah said, "I've just been handled."

"Yes, but if it is any recompense, you've been handled by the best." Rina snickered.

"I'm going back to school," she said.

"Yes, we know." Luke said.

She turned with tears in her eyes. "No, you don't understand. I'm going back to school full time. I get a second chance."

She threw her arms up and hugged first Luke, then Rina, and then she kissed Bradley.

"Mom, mom!" Bobby called.

Sarah ran to him and hugged and kissed him. "Ugh, Mom stop, what's with you? I told you, you can't kiss me when there are other people around."

"Yes, of course." Sarah said, the corner of her lips ticking up.

"My very big, grown-up boy."

"Bradley, what is wrong with mom?"

"I think she is just happy, kid. What was your news?"

"The metal detector is going nuts in this quadrant." Bobby pointed to the diorama grid.

Bradley looked at Luke. "Shovels?"

Luke nodded, "Shovels."

31

Within an hour, they had found some old coins, a few old bicycle links, but no platters. "Bobby, bring that thing over her so I can see if we can stop digging," Luke said.

"Okay, Nonc Luke. I'm sorry." Bobby said, looking a little defeated.

"What for?" Bradley asked.

"Because I made you do all that work for nothin'," Bobby said.

"It wasn't for nothing, Bobby. We are looking for answers. Whenever you look for answers, you have to be willing to find the wrong answers. The wrong answers help you find the right answers," Rina told him. "That is one thing that all scientists know."

As Rina was giving her pep talk, the metal detector started going off. "See, it might not have been in the first layer, but perhaps deeper down," Rina told Bobby.

Luke and Bradley began digging again. They kept digging until they heard a clang. "Oh, that sounded big," Sarah told Bobby.

"We got something," Luke and Bradley called to them. The hole was so deep now that one of them had to jump in the hole to continue digging.

"That's good because you are about to hit the water table and create a new pond in our backyard," Rina said, and then her mouth gaped at the huge, flat metallic object that Bradley was pulling out of the hole.

"*Mon dieu*! (My God) Bobby, go and rinse this off," Rina said as Bradley handed her the platter. "Sarah!" she continued.

"Already on my way," Sarah called back as she rushed into the house to tell Tante D that they had found her platters. Luke and Bradley were able to dig up six platters.

"This Thanksgiving is going to be beautiful!!" Tante D exclaimed, as she pulled out her silver polish. "Here, start cleaning," she told Luke before he could even wash his hands.

Bradley smiled over at Luke and mouthed, "Told you."

"Bradley, sit and polish as well. I'll make everyone some hot cider."

Bradley and Luke polished as Rina went over what she called 'Phase III of the LeBlanc Family Treasure Hunt.'

"So, what we have left to find is the fur coat, which, according to Del's information, contains the family jewels." Luke and Bradley snickered.

"Stupid middle school humor." Rina rolled her eyes.

"You two are so immature," Sarah agreed.

"What's so funny?" Bobby asked.

"Nothing!" Sarah and Rina responded together.

"I'll tell you later," Bradley whispered to him.

Rina cleared her throat. "Moving on to Phase III. What we really need is to figure out where any family furs are stored and if they have been given away," Rina mused.

All eyes turned to Tante D. "Well, I think we have a cedar closet in the *garconnière* that has some furs in it."

"Bradley and I checked the attic. We did not find it."

"You checked the main attic, but there is a secondary attic over the carriage house. Did you check that one?" Tante D asked.

"No," Sarah groaned, not anxious to go and explore the spider-infested attics again.

"No problem, Bobby and I can look for it." Bradley offered. "You just stay downstairs, so if we find it, we can let you know and you can tell the others."

Sarah looked relieved and mouthed, "Thank you!" Bradley winked at her and took Bobby to the carriage house attic.

They searched the attic for a cedar chest or armoire and found a few of them. They decided the best thing to do was to open them up and carry anything that looked like fur down to Sarah. Luke and Rina arrived as they were carrying down their third load.

"The basement has nothing of value in it," lamented Rina.

"That is because that was your lab, dear. I never put anything of value near your lab. I've learned better," Tante D said as she sashayed into the carriage house.

"You know," Sarah said as she helped Bobby with his load of coats, "I think this carriage house is adorable. I didn't realize it was so big." She went off to explore more as Tante D carefully unwrapped a package that Bradley and Bobby had gotten from the attic.

"Fur," she said and passed it to Rina. Rina patted it down and also took the metal detector to it.

"Bobby, this is the best contraption ever," Rina said.

"Thanks Tante Rina," he said, glowing with pride. "Here, why don't you pat down and I will detect."

"Sounds like a plan," Rina told him. And so it went, with Tante D unwrapping, Rina patting down and Bobby scanning for metal. When all was said and done, they had found four fur coats with items hidden in the coat linings.

Tante D and Sarah carefully undid the seams of those coats and found three gold rings with embedded stones, a necklace that looked to be diamond and sapphire, and a number of ear bobs, as Tante D called them.

Tante D had Luke and Bradley polish them up and then Sarah, Rina and she tried on all the jewelry. Tante D gave Sarah the necklace because the sapphires looked beautiful on her. She gave Luke the diamond and ruby ring to give to Rina, and then she gave Rina some emerald ear bobs. She also gave Sarah a ring to give to Bobby when he was older, for his "*belle*" as she called it. Finally, when no one was looking, she snuck the last ring to Bradley for him to "give to Sarah when the time was right."

Heading back up to bed, Tante D's parting words were, "I told you there was a treasure."

As Luke and Rina retired that night, Luke couldn't seem to keep from staring.

"What?" Rina asked.

"Nothing."

"You keep staring at me, or more specifically, my tummy."

"I just can't believe something is growing in there," Luke said.

"It is not like an alien, you know. It is not going to pop out and attack."

"I wouldn't be too sure. It is your kid. It is going to have spunk as well as a terrible voice and an even worse taste in music."

"Hey, there is nothing wrong with my taste in music!"

"Well, at least you agree on the spunk and terrible voice comments." Rina threw a pillow at him.

"I'm tired," Rina yawned.

"Oh my God, why didn't you tell me? You've been standing all day. You probably never sit down in class either. Oh no, you can't teach chemistry. You can't be around all those chemicals when you are going to have a baby!"

"Luke!"

"You need to sit down," he commanded as he dragged the reading chair over and gently pushed her down into it. "No, no, lay down, that's better," he muttered. And he yanked her out of the chair and pushed her towards the bed.

Rina's lips quirked up, "Luke!"

"Are you hungry? Did you eat enough? I should get you some more food. What do you want to eat?"

"Luke!" Rina yelled.

"What? You shouldn't be getting upset. It's bad for the baby!"

"Luke, sweetheart, you need to sit down," Rina told him and gently directed him to the chair that he had just yanked her out of.

"I ... I think I do ...I don't feel well."

"Head on your knees. Now, take a deep breath."

Luke inhaled. "Now another," she said, and Luke inhaled again.

"Much better now." Rina was about to continue when she noticed that Luke was starting to turn red. "Exhale! Exhale Luke!" He finally did.

"Now keep inhaling and exhaling."

Rina started to massage his shoulders. She straddled his lap so she could massage his shoulders, arms, and chest. Leaning over and kissing his ear, she asked, "Does that feel better?"

Luke nodded. "Keep breathing," Rina said, and she laid against his chest. "It is going to be okay. We just need to relax. Everything will be fine."

Luke's arms came around her as her head found its way to the crook of his neck. "It will all be fine," she said, and she drifted off as Luke rubbed her back.

Luke, having gained his composure, gently lifted Rina up and even more gently set her down on their bed. He removed her shoes and tugged her pants off. He smiled at all the hot pink lace with blue polka dots; Rina had the best underwear. She always wore something fun. He reached up and unbuttoned her shirt as Rina curled into her pillow. He smiled when he saw she had a matching hot pink lace bra.

He pulled out her ponytail, trying to make sure he did not snag on her many curls. Then he began to run his fingers over her scalp. Pushing his fingers into her scalp and then gently pulling on her hair as he moved his hands to the front of her scalp again. Rina moaned with pleasure. Luke moved on to her neck. Massaging it at the base of the scalp, then up and down either side of the vertebrae. From there, he moved to her shoulders, massaging her lats, the muscles between her neck and her shoulders, then the pecs down the front, avoiding her breasts to keep from getting distracted.

He moved Rina onto her belly and massaged up and down her spine. Following the lines of her ribs, and even folding her arms back to better massage the muscles on her shoulder blades. Luke then moved to her lower back and her buttocks that he massaged, using his fist to get in deep. Rina emitted another moan of pleasure. By the time Luke got to Rina's legs, he was having a difficult time thinking. He slowly massaged the back of her thighs, but when he got to the backs of her knees, the moan of need that Rina gave was so visceral that he could not continue.

He flipped her over and kissed her, deeply. His hands moved to her breasts, and she locked her legs around him. He tried to push away to move down her body, but Rina would have none of it.

Using her momentum, she flipped him onto his back and started nibbling on his neck and his nipples and then she brushed her face against his chest hair, inhaling his scent. She followed the line of his chest hair with kisses, down to his belly button, where she began to lick him, moving even further down his hard body. Soon she was licking his member up and down.

She took him fully into her mouth as she played with his 'family jewels', smiling as she heard him inhale.

Licking the edge of his head and shaking her head to make a swirling motion. Luke bowed off the bed and tried to pull her up. She resisted shaking her head, which made him even crazier. "Rina," he moaned, "please." She redoubled her efforts.

Rina could feel his entire body contracting, and she knew she was the one who did that to him. At the last moment, when she knew there was no turning back, she delicately licked the tip of his head and then pressed him between her breasts. Luke exploded, arching off the bed and yelling as he came on her breasts. Rina gave him one last lick, kissed his tummy, and then went to the bathroom to clean off and get him a towel.

32

On her way back, she heard a timid knock on the door. "Tante Rina, Nonc Luke are y'all okay?"

Luke pulled a pillow over his head, and Rina laughed. "We're fine Bobby. Nonc Luke just stubbed his toe. He's a bit of a baby. You should hear him when he actually hurts himself," Rina yelled to Bobby.

"Okay ... Nonc Luke, do you want me to get some ice for your toe?"

Rina crumpled into the chair, laughing. Luke shuddered. "No, thank you Bobby. You go back to bed and I wouldn't mind if you did not tell your mom or Mr. Bradley about this." But Bobby had already left.

"Oh, my God!"

"You're welcome," Rina said.

"You do realize that I will NEVER live this down if Bobby tells Sarah and Bradley."

"Oh, you can be sure he will tell them. Expect grief tomorrow at breakfast and then again at dinner."

"Argh! I'm too tired to think about it. You wore me out, woman," Luke said. He covered his head with his pillow and he soon fell asleep.

"You can catch me tomorrow," Rina whispered in his ear and snuggled up next to him.

The next morning Rina came awake on a wave of pleasure. 'Luke must have heard me last night,' she thought, as Luke cupped her rear and licked into her. Rolling her clit between his teeth and his tongue, Luke sucked and licked until Rina arched up from the force of her orgasm. At that exact moment, he moved up her body and plunged into her, causing a momentous second orgasm. Her sheath locked around him, and she pistoned her hips as Luke fondled her breasts and entwined his tongue with hers. Three more thrusts and it was all over. This time Rina's kiss muffled his yell.

When they were lying collapsed on each other in a sweaty heap, Rina glanced over and smiled. "What?" Luke asked.

"You're a screamer!" Rina said.

"Not usually." Luke said.

"Well, you're a screamer now and you won't be getting any other chances to test the theory on anyone else."

Luke smiled at her jealousy. "No?"

"Not if you know what's good for you. Don't forget about those dueling pistols I still have."

"You would fight for my honor?" Luke asked.

"More like shoot you in the ass," Rina said and slapped the topic of her conversation.

"Ouch!"

"Baby, what with that and your stubbed toe, you are just a wimp today."

"God, don't remind me. How will I ever face my nephew again?"

"Luke Hebert, you are blushing."

"Crap! Can't I stay in here today? We really don't have anything to do and I can make it worth your while." He gave an exaggerated leer.

"No doubt, but I'm starving, and if I don't go and cook, or at least oversee, then Sarah will do it. I need to eat, not figure out how to stash food in the trash."

"C'mon upsy-daisy," she said and reached over to pull Luke out of the bed. Instead, Luke pulled her down into bed.

"Stop that, you horny toad. I need to eat. I'm eating for two, you remember?"

"Oh, my God! I forgot!" Luke darted out of bed and pulled her toward the door. "It probably isn't good for you to be hungry. Why didn't you tell me sooner?"

"Luke."

"We can go out to eat if there is nothing down there." He pulled her out the door.

"Luke."

"I think I have some candy. What am I saying?! That is poison. You can't eat that!"

"Luke, I need to get some clothes on!"

Luke looked at Rina. She was buck naked and standing outside their bedroom door.

"That's quite a show," Bradley said. "Lucky for you, Bobby is already downstairs, or you may have scarred him for life."

"You idiot" Rina pulled her arm out of Luke's and headed to the bedroom to get a bathrobe. She came out blushing a vibrant shade of red. Luke did not look repentant. "Sorry about that, Bradley. Anytime I mention the 'B' word,me, Luke loses his mind."

"Not a problem. Nice rack, by the way!" Bradley told her.

"Hey!" Luke said, pushing Bradley forward, "Clean thoughts!"

"You're the one dragging a naked woman down the hall," Bradley said.

"My naked woman!" Luke said.

"Hey caveman, I don't belong to anybody," Rina yelled back at them.

"Wrong, see that ring? You belong to me," Luke said.

"You might want to keep her nakedness in your own cave then," Bradley smirked. Luke pushed him again. "I'm just saying," Bradley smiled. Both Luke and Bradley nearly ran into Rina, who had stopped in the middle of the hallway.

"My ring," she said, her eyes tearing up. "It's one of Tante D's heirloom rings."

"Yes, she gave it to me and I gave it to you because you are mine. I put it on you last night," Luke said. Rina was crying now and threw herself into Luke's arms.

"Ack tears," Bradley said and rushed to the kitchen.

"It is a beautiful ring," Rina said.

"Yes, and Tante D says she thinks it is an interesting metal, perhaps not gold. She said you would appreciate the ring and that you would be able to tell what it was made of."

"You got me a ring for my spectroscope!" Rina cried louder.

"This is a good thing, right?" Luke said. "I might need some man-speak translations."

"Ring good! Reward better!" Rina said.

"Really!" Luke said and started to nudge her back to the room.

"Feed baby first," Rina said.

Luke leaned down and kissed her ear. "Okay, but then I get my reward."

"You got it." Rina grinned.

$$33$$

In the kitchen, they were all gathered at the island on the bar stools. Sarah had made the coffee and was pouring it into mugs. Except for Rina, who had begrudgingly agreed to change to hot tea. Rina looked down at her belly and said, "Don't ever say I didn't do anything for you kid, all these people are witnesses to what I'm sacrificing for you."

Bobby looked at his mom and made the international sign of "Crazy."

Rina, who was apparently starving, had decided to make banana pancakes and eggs. Once she had served everyone, she ran to the cabinet for some peanut butter.

"Is that good?" Bobby asked.

"Yes, very!" Rina slathered on the peanut butter and then made a perfect bite with a piece of banana in her pancake and some peanut butter. Right when she had chewed it all together, she took a sip of hot chocolate. "Mmm, like a banana-flavored Reese's peanut butter cup. *Miamm* (Yum)," Rina.

"Ewww!" Bobby said, "That is gross."

Rina pushed her plate towards him. "Wanna try?"

"Okay." Bobby cut off a piece with banana and peanut butter and then swallowed some of his hot chocolate with it. "Mom, this is pretty good."

"I'm glad sweetie, but pretty soon Tante Rina is going to want some weird stuff."

"Why is that, darling?" Tante D sashayed in.

"Cuz she has a bun in the oven," Bobby told her.

"Bobby!"

"What? Mr. Bradley says she is cooking a baby in there." Bobby pointed to Rina's stomach.

"*Cherie! T'es en famille!*" (Darling, you are pregnant) Tante D gave her a big hug.

"Mom said she is going to like to eat yucky stuff, but I had some of her banana pancakes with peanut butter, and it was good."

"Actually, Rina has always eaten her pancakes with peanut butter, especially the banana ones," Tante D said. "Although," she continued tracking Rina's movements, "she never added pickle relish before."

All eyes turned to Rina, who was spooning sweet relish onto her pancakes. "What? I thought it would give it a nice crunch. Wanna try some Bobby?" she asked.

Bobby held his lips together and said, "No, thank you."

All eyes stayed on Rina as she started pouring syrup on her pancakes. "Perfect," she said. She started eating her plate enthusiastically when she noticed her untouched eggs. Her eyes darted to everyone else who had started eating again as she added a piece of egg to her perfect-bite eating strategy.

"That is soo gross, Tante Rina. Can I take a picture?"

Rina laughed, "No! you can't, Bobby. Can we please talk about something else?"

Bobby had a hard time taking his eyes off her.

Bradley whispered, "It is hard to take your eyes off it, isn't it? It is kinda like a train wreck. Too gross to look away."

"*Changeons le suject*! Please! Can we talk about something else ...anything else?" Rina asked.

"Ah, Ah ..." Bobby tried to think through his fascination, "Nonc Luke, how is your toe?" Rina's last mouthful came spurting out as she coughed and coughed to try to catch her breath.

"Super Gross!!!" Bobby said, completely impressed with his thoroughly disgusting aunt.

"I'm sorry." Rina wiped her mouth, "Yes, Luke, how is your toe?"

Luke turned a bright shade of red. "Would you like some Tabasco for your eggs, dear?" Luke said, trying desperately to change the subject.

"You hurt your toe, Luke?" Sarah asked, concerned.

"I'm fine," Luke said, "not a scratch on me."

"Well, that is not strictly true." Rina said. Luke pulled on a curl. "Oww! Stop that."

"I will if you will," Luke said. Rina stuck her tongue out at Luke.

"Why do I have a feeling we are missing something?" Bradley said.

"It was nothing." Luke said.

Rina looked affronted, and Luke pulled another curl. "Will you quit?!"

"You should've heard him, Mr. Bradley." Bobby explained, while Luke waited for the comprehension to dawn.

"He yelled like someone had just broken his leg or something. I rushed down to make sure he was okay. Tante Rina said he was just being a big baby because he just stubbed his toe, and then she started laughing at him. I don't think that was very nice, Tante Rina." Bobby scolded her with his eyes.

"Sorry." Rina said, obviously trying to keep from laughing. "I asked Nonc Luke if he wanted me to get him some ice." Bobby continued. A squeaking sound came out of Rina as she tried desperately to keep from laughing. "Cuz you know you wouldn't want it to swell," Bobby said.

Rina collapsed into giggles. She couldn't stop laughing and laid her head on the island, pounding her hand next to her. She tried stopping, but every time she did, she would look at Luke's bright red face and then start laughing again.

"Yes, well, all better now." Luke said, which sent Rina into peals of laughter.

"I'm surprised," Bobby said, wondering what was wrong with his new aunt. "I mean, you really yelled."

"Told you. You're a screamer." Rina tried to whisper to Luke.

"Oh, my God!" Sarah said, just catching on.

"What?" Bradley said, and then it dawned on him. "Good Lord, between the screaming and the Lady Godiva episodes, this house is starting to get an 'M' rating."

"Huh?" Bobby said.

"Never mind," Sarah told him. "You just get ready for school. We will be leaving in 20 minutes. Any extra time you have, you can spend in the playroom."

"Yes!" Bobby said and ran off to prepare.

"Children," Tante D, who had been having her morning tea in the dining room, called to them. Summoned, they all got up and went to the dining room. "I've been thinking, perhaps it would be better if the newlywed couple could move to the carriage house. It would give them their necessary privacy," Tante D said. "What do you think?"

"I love that idea Tante D. I can prepare it over the Thanksgiving holiday," Rina said. "Nonsense. I'll have some workers over today to move all of your things. Now, let me see your ring, dear."

Rina showed them her new ring, and they oohed and ahhed over it for a while. "So, off to the carriage house with you," Tante D said. As they were leaving, they heard her mutter, "That way we can all get a decent night's sleep. God, what a screamer."

"Kill me now," Luke said.

Rina laughed, "C'mon Tarzan. I need to pack my valuables. If Tante D wants something done, she will get it done today, so you can expect to be moved in by the time we get back."

"Fine, but tonight I will make you scream."

"Not a problem. We have sprayed insulation and double paned Hurricane glass on the carriage house. But I'll hold you to it." Rina smiled as she kissed him on the cheek.

About the Author

Growing up in French Louisiana, Gigi was always a reader. But writing also played a role in her life once she began teaching. She worked with the National Writing project as a teacher and then helped to run a program as a professor. She participated in several Nanowrimo experiences (write a novel in a month) throughout the years. However, after she retired in November 2022, she finally listened to her inner voice and challenged herself to become a published writer.

Important to note: Since Gigi now lives abroad, she often uses her writing to connect to her home and experiences in Louisiana. Most of the restaurants and food in her work are not fictional places, although some of them have closed. Go eat there ... you will appreciate the Louisiana cuisine. Coming from a French Louisiana background, Gigi also includes the occasional French word or expression. She plans to create a Louisiana French bookmark to highlight her most used Cajun/Creole vocabulary.

Also by Gigi Hodge

Louisiana L'Amour Series

Learning to Love: Book 1
Dance of Love: Book 2
Thrown into Love: Book 3
Noël in Love: Book 4
Storm of Love (Novella)
Louisiana L'Amour Omnibus

Louisiana Small Town Romance

The Magic of Chemistry

The Babineaux Brothers

Bayou Catfish

Acknowledgements

No author is an island. It takes a team to pull together a book. I want to thank mine. So, thanks to my beta readers, Rebecca Klug and H. Stone whose insights have been invaluable. I want to thank Lois Carter Crawford for giving me a free line edit, best author gift ever. I also want to thank the All Write Well team for their support and instruction to help me learn how to move from being a hobby writer into a published author.